THE PARTY KILLER

ALSO BY HUGH PENTECOST

THE PARTY KILLER

A JULIAN QUIST MYSTERY NOVEL

Hugh Pentecost

DODD, MEAD & COMPANY
NEW YORK

Published by Dodd, Mead & Company, Inc.
79 Madison Avenue, New York, N.Y. 10016
Distributed in Canada by
McClelland and Stewart Limited, Toronto
Manufactured in the United States of America
First Edition

Library of Congress Cataloging-in-Publication Data

Pentecost, Hugh
    The party killer.

    I. Title.
PS3531.H442P27   1985   813'.54   85-16076
ISBN 0-396-08692-6

PART
ONE

1

"The best laid plans of mice and men," Julian Quist reminded himself later, have a way of stumbling over the most unexpected twists of fate. The public relations firm of Julian Quist Associates runs with Swiss-watch efficiency if the unexpected will let it alone. But on a weekend in June the unexpected had itself a field day. It started with an upset stomach and ended with a murder.

The upset stomach belonged to the heavyweight boxing champion of the world, who had nothing whatever to do with the events that followed, except that by eating some raw oysters in a month without an *R* in it, the resulting stomachache forced him to delay the defense of his title by three days. As a result of that, Julian Quist Associates had to alter their schedules. Dan Garvey, the number-one associate, a former star professional football player, had been set to cover the big fight and also the opening of Larry Lewis's fabulous new vacation resort in southern New England. The delay of the fight forced Garvey to choose between it and the opening of Rainbow Hill. Being the sports expert at Julian Quist's, it was decided that he would cover the fight and Quist himself would go to Rainbow Hill. The Fates had played their first joker, but Quist had no way of guessing that he was being projected into a life-threatening situation.

Dealing with famous people and promoting their fortunes was everyday work for Quist. He wasn't awed by big names. He had come across too many skeletons in too many closets in his time. There was one unusual thing about Larry Lewis, however. He hung his skeletons right out

3

front for everyone to see and enjoy. Most prominent among those skeletons were four glamorous ex-wives who had all agreed to be guests at the opening of Rainbow Hill. Only an "original" like Larry Lewis could have gathered four ex-wives under one roof in a friendly conclave. They, too, were headed, unknowingly, toward violence and death.

Quist had known three of the wives professionally, if not socially. The number-one wife was Sandra Ames, often called the first lady of Broadway and Hollywood and compared with such stars as Helen Hayes, Katharine Cornell, and Judith Anderson on the stage, and with Joan Crawford, Carole Lombard, and Vivien Leigh in Hollywood. As Sandra was still beautiful in her late fifties, Quist had promoted a revival of *Medea* that she had brought to Broadway, and he had found her a gracious and charming lady. Number two was Beverly Jadwin, "the girl with the million-dollar legs," who still had the bald-headed men in the front rows gasping with delight when she did her thing in a Broadway musical. Number three was Patti Payne, blonde, brash, an acid-tongued comic whose boisterous laugh had delighted millions of television fans over the years. Number four was Glenda Forrest, cut out of another piece of cloth, heiress to the Forrest oil millions, unknown to the public, unlike her predecessors, except as a kind of sexy dollar sign.

And the man who had captured these four glamorous ladies over the years? A kind of Laurence Olivier, or Clark Gable, or Burt Reynolds? About as far from that notion as you can imagine. Larry Lewis stood about five feet five inches tall, reaching only to Quist's breastbone when they faced each other. Fifty years ago he'd been a child star in the movies, playing a sort of Peck's bad boy in two-reel comedies. He'd graduated to playing character juveniles, and from that to a singing and dancing career that earned him millions of dollars and had people all over the world loving him. Now over sixty, he was still at the top of the heap. People old enough to remember compared him with Bojangles Robinson, Fred Astaire, Gene Kelly, and Ray Bolger. The mischievous kid's face was deeply lined now, but those lines had been etched there by good humor and laughter.

How had this diminutive clown attracted so many glamorous ladies? It was Quist's theory that the mischievous kid in the man aroused their maternal instincts, and then when they tried to coddle him they found themselves captured by a whirlwind lover. Though none of the marriages had worked, the separations must not have been nasty, or how could all four of them be gathered under the same roof to celebrate Larry's latest toy—a million-dollar vacation resort?

Rainbow Hill had been a country inn for many years before Larry Lewis bought it, refurbished it, transformed its golf course into a championship layout, built indoor and outdoor swimming pools, cut ski trails and horseback riding trails into the hills surrounding it, and added tennis courts and squash courts to the things it had to offer.

"I always dreamed of a place like this," Larry had told Dan Garvey, "and I finally got rich enough to buy one and fix it up exactly as I wanted it."

It wasn't just a high salary that had made Larry rich. He'd been shrewd enough to always have "a piece of the show" on Broadway, a share of the profits in Hollywood, and endless payments for reruns on television. He could afford a million-dollar toy like Rainbow Hill. Certainly the last thing he thought of, as the grand opening approached, was murder.

The lobby of the gracious old inn was crowded with familiar faces from films, Broadway, and television when Quist arrived on a Saturday afternoon, the afternoon of *the* day. Quist himself was not unknown to many of the famous guests. Tall, blond, almost Greek-god handsome, he had acted for many of these people in his professional capacity.

5

At the desk, where he registered, he encountered Bobby Crown, Larry's business manager, a bright-faced little man only an inch or two taller than his boss.

"Had my eye out for you, Mr. Quist. Larry's been expecting you."

Quist looked around. "Who's who in show business," he said.

"Larry's taken over the guest cottage at the foot of the back garden," Bobby said. "A little more privacy there than in this main building. He asked me to send you down there when you were settled in."

"Foot of the garden?"

"Just go through those French doors over there. The garden's there. You'll see the cottage at the other end, stage left."

Someone waved to Quist from across the lobby, and he saw that it was Sandra Ames, Larry's wife number one. He waved back. "The exes all here?" he asked Bobby.

"In spades, and each one able to turn heads. That Sandra's really something, isn't she? She doesn't tell her age, but she and Larry were married forty years ago."

The room assigned to Quist looked out over that back garden, and he could see the guest cottage at the other end of it, stage left. When he'd unpacked and hung up his clothes, Quist went back downstairs and walked out into the garden, headed for the cottage. Before he reached it, the front door opened and Larry Lewis appeared, beckoning to him urgently.

"Get in here before half the reporters in the world swarm down on us," Larry said. He ushered Quist into the cottage, where it appeared they were not alone. A beautiful red-haired woman wearing tailored white slacks and a scarlet blouse was smiling at them. Quist had never seen her before except in photographs, but he didn't have to be told that this was ex-wife number four, Glenda Forrest. She smiled at Quist charmingly as Larry introduced them.

6

"You're a household word at home," Glenda said. "My father talks about you all the time."

"Oh?"

"You're not one of his favorite people, Mr. Quist. He never forgets anyone who dares to say no to him."

"Catch me up," Larry said. "You said no to old man Forrest? I don't believe it, you know. Your head is still attached to your body."

"Daddy wanted Julian—may I first-name you, Mr. Quist—to promote his new company. Julian refused. A Forrest never forgets!"

"You turned down Forrest money, Julian?" Larry said. "You and I must be the only members of the club."

"Forrest Industries were embarking on the manufacture of nuclear weapons," Quist said. "I didn't choose to be a party to selling them."

"Daddy's waiting for the right moment to stab you in the back," Glenda said.

"Well, he isn't here for the party, so you're safe for now, Julian," Larry said. "Look, Julian, I'm sorry Dan couldn't be here, but I couldn't be happier with his substitute. Nobody can handle the press better than you. But you won't have to worry about that till tomorrow. The party tonight will speak for itself. Just know that you can't buy a meal or a drink while you're here. As far as you're concerned, everything is on the house."

At that moment the door to the cottage burst open as if it had been hit by a runaway tank, and a big athletic-looking man charged into the room. He appeared not to see Quist or Glenda. He rushed to Larry Lewis, grabbed him by the shoulders, and lifted him off the floor so that they were eyeball to eyeball.

"I warned you, you miserable little creep!" the man shouted. "Stop sniffing around Glenda, or I'll break your ass and both your arms and legs at the same time."

Larry Lewis didn't struggle at all, held up in space off the

7

floor. "Let me remind you, Paul," he said, "that you're talking in front of a lady—not that you'd recognize one without being told. The gentleman is Julian Quist—Paul Powers."

Powers slammed Larry down onto the floor, and the little man seemed to tap-dance away from him.

"This is a last warning, buster!" Powers said. "Keep your grimy paws off Glenda, or you'll wind up in an emergency ward somewhere."

Glenda's dark eyes were blazing. "Damn you, Paul!" she said, and turned and literally ran out of the cottage into the garden.

Powers was breathing hard as if he'd been running a marathon. He started toward Larry. "Maybe I better give you a practice going-over, creep," he said.

"Easy does it," Quist said, stepping between the two men.

"You asking for trouble, pretty boy?" Powers said.

"Do you insist on finding out how well I can handle it?" Quist asked.

Powers glared down at Larry. "You've got the message," he said. "There won't be another warning." He turned and strode out of the room, out of the cottage, slamming the door behind him.

"So bloweth the big wind," Larry said, grinning at Quist. "You think you could have handled him, Julian?"

"I'm not unhappy that he didn't ask me to try it," Quist said. "Are you in the process of reviving your romance with Glenda?"

"You don't have any ex-wives, do you, Julian?"

"No."

"It's a relationship that can go one of two ways," Larry said. "It can be hate, which you see all around you in separated couples, or it can be a pleasant, relaxed, uncomplicated friendship. Sandra Ames and I were married when we were both kids, divorced years ago. Separate careers that kept us apart. There'd been no time for whatever it is that makes a marriage work. We parted without hard feelings. We just couldn't make it together. But over the years I've been able to help her with her career, hold her hand when the going was rough. We've been good friends all this time, no hard feelings, no blaming the other one for what went wrong. I guess I learned something from it?"

"How to get rid of your next three wives?" Quist asked.

"That's kind of a snotty question, pal, but I suppose it's justified," Larry said, smiling his impish smile. "Beverly Jadwin and I were married when we were starring together in *Changing Times* on Broadway, a long-running musical like *Oklahoma!, South Pacific, Guys and Dolls*. But after it closed Bev got a shot at Hollywood, I got another Broadway show. After that it was vice versa, I on the Coast, Bev back on Broadway. I guess I wasn't cut out to be a monk, Bev wasn't a nun. We were faithful to each other while we were together, but during those long separations—well, it was fun while it lasted but it just came to an end. There was no reason to be anything but friends, it just hadn't worked out. Then there was Patti Payne—"

"Pardon the impertinence," Quist said, "but Patti was in her early twenties when you married. You were in your fifties."

"I could still run a pretty fast mile, chum," Larry said with that twisted, infectious grin of his. "Trouble was, Patti couldn't decide whether she wanted to be an actress or a housewife. One day she'd choose one, and as soon as she'd made the choice she'd decide on the other. In the end we both went the way of all flesh—but we stayed friends."

"That seems to be a special genius of yours."

"Genius or luck, I'm glad of it either way," Larry said. "That brings me to Glenda, the lady Powers is so concerned about. Don't remind me that she was nineteen and I was sixty. I could *still* run a pretty fast mile. The trouble there was my life. She wanted me to give up acting, retire, buy a ranch somewhere, and settle down to raise a family."

"She could afford a life of leisure," Quist said.

"I forgive you for that," Larry said. "Believe it or not, I'd made enough out of Broadway, films, and television to buy most of her old man's oil wells! He hated me for that. He'd had to work hard for what he had. I'd just tap-danced my way to money. Too easy to suit him."

"Maybe he didn't realize that singing and tap-dancing your way to millions might have been just a little harder than digging a hole in the ground and striking oil," Quist said. "Is the elephant man who just left here Glenda's current boyfriend?"

Larry laughed. "He's Fred Forrest's candidate, not Glenda's."

"But you've invited him here for your party."

Larry shrugged. "Glenda wanted to come, and I wanted her to come. Forrest threatened to do me some kind of harm if his daughter came here without Powers."

"So you knuckled under?"

"I wanted Glenda to come. It was part of my scheme for the party tonight—to have all my ex-wives on hand to help me celebrate. They all wanted to come. So I invited Powers so Forrest wouldn't have an excuse for doing something that might spoil the evening. I'm surrounded by friends, Julian, for this shindig." He grinned. "You were here, weren't you, when I needed you?"

A few hours later Quist stood at the edge of the ballroom floor with Bobby Crown, watching the party begin. He thought he'd never seen anything quite like it, perhaps because there had never been anything quite like it. To begin with, not five of the two hundred guests were less than famous. Quist knew many of them personally and almost all of them by sight. They all seemed to know each

10

other and be on a wonderfully relaxed and pleasant trip together.

"'Good old buddy-buddy' time," Bobby Crown said.

"And the clothes!" Quist said. "Those ladies make a Paris fashion show look like an attic sale. You know what gets me, Bobby? Those are all primarily show-business people, with all the envies and jealousies, the throat-cutting impulses for which they're famous, yet everyone seems to love everyone."

Bobby nodded. "The Larry Lewis magic, I call it," he said. "Almost all these people have worked with Larry over his fifty-year career—as actors, directors, writers, choreographers. It says something for him, doesn't it, that I've never heard anyone say that he ever tried to sink a hatchet into anyone's head? He has shared where sharing was called for, he's taken a back seat when it was someone else's night, he has always helped people when they had a run of bad luck. I don't know anyone in our business who has his kind of reputation."

"Unique for someone at the top of the heap," Quist said.

"In spades," Bobby said.

Charlie Horner's famous dance band kept people on the move, and there were bars and buffets everywhere you turned. It took skill and planning to make anything look so pleasantly casual. Yet careful organization began to appear. At a break in the dancing, Larry called for attention and introduced Bud Taylor, a new and very popular young singer. Taylor sang a couple of numbers and the guests loved him.

A little later Larry took the stand again. "We're honored to have the queen of Hollywood with us, the greatest of them all, Sandra Ames. Say hello to her!"

There were no sly remarks about "my ex-wife." Larry held out his hand to her as Sandra came up the steps to the bandstand. Then he took a few steps back and bowed to her. It was her moment. That still-gorgeous woman ex-

11

pressed her delight at being there with so many friends, wished Larry the best of luck with Rainbow Hill, and let him guide her down off the stand to thunderous applause.

At the next break Larry took the stand again. "One of the most important talents in show business is the ability to steal good material from other performers and not get sued for it! You have to know enough, though, only to steal from the really great ones." Laughter and applause. "Twenty-five years ago Bev Jadwin and I stole from that incomparable couple, Fred Astaire and Ginger Rogers. I wonder how many of you remember *Changing Times* and how shamelessly Bev and I copied Fred and Ginger?"

He held out his hand and Bev Jadwin, dark, svelte, smiling, came up to him out of the crowd. Charlie Horner's band began to play "Top Hat, White Tie, and Tails." Larry and Bev took off, and Quist watched, amazed. The ugly little man was suddenly all grace, his flying feet tapping so brilliantly it almost seemed they were giving you the words to the song.

"Some copy," Bobby said. "Now they're ready for someone else to copy them."

"The girl with the million-dollar legs still has them," Quist said.

Larry and Bev could have held the party all night, but they stopped after the one number, and the general dancing was resumed. Then, once again, Larry took the stand.

"You think Bev and I stole from the best. Well, Patti Payne and I did some stealing later on from the best— George Burns and Gracie Allen."

Patti Payne, ex-wife number three, came up from the audience, long blonde hair hanging down below her shoulders. She and Larry went into a routine that may not have been stolen from Burns and Allen but was certainly based on their formula. It convulsed the audience for a good ten minutes.

When the dancing started again, Quist asked Bobby Crown what was planned for "number four."

"Glenda? Larry wouldn't ask a nonprofessional to perform," Bobby said.

Quist had been watching for Glenda most of the evening but hadn't caught a glimpse of her. Neither had he seen anything of the large Mr. Powers. The muscleman had evidently had his way with the lady.

Quist danced with a couple of the women he knew, and then at about four in the morning the orchestra began to play "Good Night, Ladies," and the party was over. The guests, exhausted by pleasure, drifted to their various quarters.

Quist went to bed and slept from the moment his head hit the pillow. He was wakened, almost knocked out of bed, by a violent explosion. Quist sat up, saw that it was daylight, glanced at his wristwatch. It was a quarter to seven.

Now he heard the sound of shouting voices and one or two shrill screams. He got up and went to the window, aware that the voices were coming from the back garden.

Down at the bottom of the garden, Larry Lewis's little guest cottage was a blazing inferno. People who were obviously part of the Inn's crew were milling around, along with a few guests in varying degrees of undress. No one was getting anywhere near the cottage. It was a fiery hell.

Feeling suddenly sick at the pit of his stomach, Quist began to dress. No one sleeping in that cottage could have survived what had happened there.

2

It was bedlam down in the lobby and out in the garden at the rear. People were streaming out of their rooms, everyone asking everyone else the same question: "What happened?" Quist, elbowed and shoved by strangers, reached the lobby on the main floor. Last night, dressed for the party, veneer in place, he had at least known who almost everyone was. Now, with makeup removed, hair disheveled, eyes blurred by sleep and perhaps too much alcohol earlier on, most of them were strangers.

No one could have slept through that monster explosion and the screaming and yelling that followed it. Somewhere in the distance the town's fire siren was sounding. Help wasn't likely to arrive in time to do much more than pour water on the embers. No one was in charge out in the garden, although the staff members seemed to be trying to stop people from getting too close to the flames. They were doing what they could to prevent hopeless heroics.

"My God, they're just letting him burn to death!" a woman's voice said next to Quist.

He turned and found himself facing Sandra Ames, Larry's first wife and "the Queen of Hollywood." Her face was ash gray, and without makeup she looked her age. She reached out to Quist as though she needed help.

"You're his friend, Quist! Why aren't you doing something?"

He put his arm around her shoulders and held her shaking body close. "Do what, lady?"

"You can't just stand and stare while a man is roasted alive!"

"You can't even get close, let alone get in," Quist said.

A siren was coming closer. The local fire company was arriving. Men shouted commands. There were evidently some hydrants near the main building, but the firemen had difficulty getting hoses through the hysterical spectators and close enough to the blaze to get water to it. People had to be shoved and pushed away; men shouted orders that no one seemed to hear or want to obey. Quist managed to move the now-weeping Sandra Ames over to one side.

"He was so gay tonight," she said, "so very much at his best! How could this happen to him?"

"We don't know for certain that he was there," Quist said.

"Where else? That's where he was living. He was there, probably with some broad if he played it as usual. No one deserves to die that way, Quist."

They were joined by Bobby Crown. He looked as if some animal had clawed fresh lines in his face, which was fish-belly white.

"Go back in the hotel, Sandra. He wouldn't want you to see—whatever there is to see," Bobby said.

"He wouldn't desert me if I was in there," Sandra said. "I won't desert him."

"Smoking in bed, I suppose," a man's voice said.

"You crazy, Mike?" Bobby Crown said. "To begin with, Larry doesn't smoke! And did you hear—and feel—that explosion? There was enough power behind that to blow up the Empire State Building!"

Quist turned and recognized Mike Reid, a Hollywood leading man. "It isn't just a fire, Mike," he said. "Damn near threw me out of bed in the other building. It looks as if someone was out to get Larry with a bomb."

"And got him," Bobby said, his voice harsh.

State police were suddenly everywhere, ordering people out of the garden. The fire company had to be given room to work freely. There was danger of the fire spreading to the

15

main building. The crowd moved back toward the Inn, Quist still supporting Sandra with an arm around her shoulder.

"We're going to need you, Julian," Bobby Crown said. "The press corps from the whole damn world is going to be snowing us under in the next hour. You know them better and will know better how to handle them than anyone else here."

"We haven't anything to give them until the police and the firemen come up with some answers," Quist said. He looked down at Sandra's tear-stained face. "You have any idea who could have hated him this much, Sandra?"

She shook her head. "He didn't make enemies—not this kind of enemy," she said. "I'm here, and his three other ex-wives are here, to help him celebrate. Does that kind of man have deadly enemies?"

"Men who wanted a woman Larry wanted," Quist said. He was thinking of the large Paul Powers a few hours back, lifting Larry up off the floor as if he were a rag doll and threatening to break his arms and legs.

"I don't keep track of his current love life," Sandra said.

"Business enemies?" Quist asked Bobby.

Bobby shrugged. "He bought this place outright, cash on the barrelhead. As far as I know, there were no other bidders. Professionally, there was nothing very complicated. He bargained for top salary, but he made profits for the people who paid him."

"As far as other actors, performers, are concerned, no one had a reputation for being more generous, more helpful, than Larry," Sandra said.

"A pretty ugly question, Bobby," Quist said, "but who inherits his fortune now?"

"Would you believe cancer research, lung disease research, a hospital for crippled children? That's it."

"No people, even modest amounts?" Quist asked.

16

"Larry was a pay-as-you-go guy," Bobby said. "He settled an annuity on you long ago, didn't he, Sandra?"

"Thirty-five years ago," Sandra said. "I'll never have to go to the old actors' home. I know he settled something on Bev Jadwin later, and after that, Patti Payne. I don't know about Glenda. Lord knows she didn't need money."

"Would you believe her favorite charity—a home for stray dogs," Bobby said.

"So no one profits from this financially?"

"No one."

"Then why?"

"Some crazy person filled with just plain crazy hate," Bobby said.

Time moved slowly as far as any kind of answers were concerned. The fire was out as far as the hot flames were concerned, but thick, dark smoke indicated that embers were still burning.

Bobby's prophecy about the press came true promptly, however. Within half an hour of the explosion, reporters from local papers were on hand, kept away from the cottage by the police, demanding answers that no one had yet. The national media, with its cameras and microphones, came a little later. Reporters from major newspapers began to arrive at the private airport Larry had built at the edge of his property. There was no official statement to give them so far, but there were enough celebrities on hand to give them a field day of sorts.

Quist was in the Inn's business office, which was in an area behind the front desk, waiting with Bobby Crown for some word from the state police. It came a little after ten o'clock in the person of Captain Ed Shannon, tall, fair-haired, tight-lipped, with very cold blue eyes.

"I understand you're the Inn's public relations man," he said to Quist when Bobby introduced him.

17

"I was hired by Larry Lewis to be that," Quist said.

"I'm going to tell you what we know, which isn't much," Shannon said. "I'm also going to tell you what you can give out to the press and what you must hold back. Understood?"

Quist nodded.

"To begin with," Shannon said, "we think there were two people in that cottage when the bomb hit. It was a bomb. No oil or gas fixtures to account for the explosion from normal causes. The medical examiner thinks there were a man and a woman in the cottage. We assume the man was Larry Lewis, not because there's any way to identify what's left of him, but because that's where he was quartered. The two people were so ripped to pieces by the bomb and then charred and destroyed by the fire that there's no way to identify them—no fingerprinting possible. Maybe there can be some sort of dental identification, but the medical examiner thinks not. Our first unanswered question is, of course, who was the woman? Did Lewis share the cottage with some woman, Crown?"

"I don't know how to answer that. We haven't been in residence very long, you know. I can only tell you that Larry has shared the cottage with more than one lady and planned to go on doing so."

"You don't know who was with him last night?"

"No notion," Bobby said. "He stayed at the party, here in the Inn, till just after four. He said goodnight to me and took off. He didn't have a lady with him, but then all he had to do was to arrange to have her meet him there."

"So it comes down to checking on who's missing," Shannon said. "Guests have been ordered not to leave until the police have a statement from them."

"The lady wouldn't have to have been a registered guest," Bobby said. "There were local people at the party." He gave the trooper a bitter smile. "Larry's been in town a

18

couple of months, you know, preparing for the grand opening. It would be out of character if he hadn't found himself a woman somewhere in the neighborhood."

"If she's local she'll turn up missing," Shannon said. "The bomb squad tells us there was enough TNT-type explosive used to blow up a city block. So far, there is no way to tell if it was thrown in a window, or planted during the evening and set to go off with a timer, or detonated by remote control when the bomber was sure his intended victim, or victims, were where he wanted them to be." Shannon's mouth twitched at the corners. "You don't carry that kind of explosive around just for the hell of it. This bombing had to be planned well in advance. Either of you want to name any enemy Lewis had?"

"I happened to be present when someone threatened him yesterday afternoon," Quist said. He described the scene with Paul Powers.

"Maybe we should have a talk with him," Shannon said. He turned to the trooper who'd come in with him and remained standing at the door. "Pick him up, Joe."

The trooper left.

"Interesting thing is that because of his threats in the cottage I kept looking for him all night at the party. Never saw him. I never saw Glenda Forrest either. I supposed she and Powers were off somewhere. Powers, according to Larry, was Fred Forrest's choice for his daughter's hand in marriage."

Shannon's cold eyes narrowed. "Could Lewis have been having a fling with his ex-wife—just for auld lang syne?"

"I don't think so," Bobby said. "One thing about Larry, when he was through with a relationship, he was through with it."

"And yet four ex-wives were here at the party. How 'through' is that?" Shannon asked.

"Through," Bobby said. "Through and friends."

19

"It's not that way in my world," Shannon said.

The door to the office opened. The trooper stationed there had gone to look for Powers. Quist thought he had suddenly lost his mind.

"*Larry!*" Bobby Crown shouted.

Larry Lewis, his ugly face looking as if it were carved out of rock, stood in the entryway.

"You Captain Shannon?" he asked.

The big trooper stared at Larry as though he, too, were dreaming.

"I thought you might want to talk to me," Larry said. "As you can see, the rumor of my death is somewhat exaggerated."

Bobby Crown rushed to Larry and threw his arms around him. "Larry! Larry!" he kept saying, over and over. After a moment Larry edged his way out of Bobby's embrace.

"Better knock it off, pal," he said, "or the captain may think you're queer."

"But Larry! They found what was left of a man and a woman out there in the cottage. We thought, naturally—"

"You *are* Larry Lewis?" Captain Shannon asked.

"Can you imagine anyone else looking like me?" Larry said, his voice sardonic. "I haven't the faintest idea who the man could have been out there in the cottage. Unfortunately, I think I know who the woman is—or was."

"Who, Larry?" Bobby asked.

Larry was facing Captain Shannon. "I think the lady in the cottage was my former wife, Glenda Forrest."

"Oh my God!" Bobby said.

"You have some reason for thinking that, not having seen what's left of her?" Shannon asked.

"I have a reason," Larry said. "She asked for the use of my cottage, and I told her to help herself. I had other plans for myself."

"Other plans?"

"To spend the night with a lady somewhere else. I wasn't going to be in the cottage myself, so I told Glenda it was all hers."

"And the man with her?"

"I haven't the foggiest," Larry said.

"You don't know?"

"Do I have to have a translator?"

Shannon's pale eyes were frosty. "Suppose you start at the beginning," he said. "Your ex-wife, Glenda Forrest, asked for the use of your cottage. By the way, isn't her name Glenda Lewis—your ex-wife?"

"She took back her maiden name, legally, when we were divorced," Larry said. "Incidentally, Glenda didn't ask me for the use of my cottage. She wanted a room somewhere other than the one in which she was registered. There wasn't an empty broom closet left in the Inn. But I wasn't planning to be in the cottage, so I told her it was hers for the night."

"Why did she want to change rooms?"

"You say there's a dead man in the cottage," Larry said, giving his shoulders a little shrug.

"If she wanted to have an affair with someone, why couldn't it be in the room that was assigned to her?" Shannon asked.

"Her father has always wanted to run her life," Larry said. "He's chosen a new husband for her, guy named Powers. Because Glenda planned to come here to my party, her old man and Powers decided she still had a yen for me. The old man wangled an invitation for Powers. Glenda had plans for herself, and she had to go undercover or Powers would be spying. So she needed a room other than the one he'd be watching."

"She never did show up at the party, or Powers either, for that matter," Quist said.

21

"She was in my cottage with the man she was interested in," Larry said. "Powers was probably looking for her. She'd given him the slip."

"I understand you did acts with two of your ex-wives," Shannon said. "Your number one got a special introduction. Wasn't anything planned for Glenda Forrest?"

"She wasn't a performer," Larry said. "She was just there as an old friend—God help her."

"I still want to know who the man with her in the cottage was," Shannon said.

"I still can't tell you," Larry said. "I didn't ask her and she didn't volunteer his name."

"You weren't curious?"

"Sure I was, but it was none of my business."

"So you were with someone somewhere else," Shannon said. "You'll need that for an alibi. What's her name?"

"That's none of your business," Larry said.

"Sooner or later you're going to need her to testify for you."

"Not until you can prove I'm the mad bomber," Larry said.

The office door opened and the trooper who'd been sent to find Powers came in. "I've got your man outside, Captain," he said.

"Bring him in," Shannon said.

"Wait!" Larry said. "Let me duck out of sight for a minute. It may be helpful if he doesn't know I'm still around." Without waiting for Shannon to reply, Larry opened a door at the back of the office and stepped into what was obviously a bathroom.

Shannon nodded to the trooper, who went out into the hall and came back with Powers. The big man saw Quist and his smile was mocking: "I thought I could count on you to set the hounds on my trail, Quist. So, Captain, what can I do for you? I can't help you name the person who killed that miserable little Lewis and the woman who was sick enough to go for him."

"I have reason to believe 'that woman' was someone who matters to you, Mr. Powers. I think she was Glenda Forrest."

The big man's knees seemed to buckle. "You must be crazy."

"She was in the cottage with a lover," Shannon said.

"Never! She never went back to that Lewis creep!"

"It wasn't Lewis," Shannon said.

The bathroom door opened and Larry came back into the office. "Surprise!" he said.

"Lewis!" Powers said, his voice wavering.

"Sorry to disappoint you, pal," Larry said. "Unfortunately, the captain is right. Glenda was in my cottage with some other guy when someone let go with a bomb. Could it have been you, thinking she was there with me?"

Powers reached for the back of a chair and braced himself on it. "You're sure it's Glenda?" he asked Shannon.

"Sure. Not a hundred percent, but sure," Shannon said.

"Oh, brother!" Powers lowered his head, and for a moment Quist thought there were going to be tears.

"Do you know who her dentist is?" Shannon asked. "It's just possible a dental chart could help us make certain."

Powers raised his head and looked past the captain at Larry. "You set her up! You framed her! What happened? Did she say no to you once too often?"

"You see what I mean about an alibi, Lewis?" Shannon said.

"No one would ever believe this creep," Larry said.

"When Mr. Forrest gets through with you, buster, the whole damn world will believe," Powers said.

"According to Mr. Quist, you weren't at the party last night," Shannon said.

"I was there early," Powers said. "When Glenda didn't

show, I went looking for her. I never dreamed she was with this punk in his cabin, never thought of looking there."

"Larry was pretty public for quite a few hours at the party," Quist said. "He was master of ceremonies, did a couple of special routines, was never out of my sight till almost four o'clock. Neither you nor Glenda ever appeared."

"He was probably too busy setting up a bomb to explode when I turned in," Larry said.

"Damn fool!" Powers said. "If I was setting up a bomb at your cottage, wouldn't I have seen that Glenda was there with someone?"

"All right, I've had enough of these accusations," Shannon said. "I want written statements from both of you; written, sworn to, and signed!"

And two hundred other guests, Quist thought.

There was a small office off the one Shannon was using, and while Shannon was listening to Powers's statement, dictated to a trooper with a stenotype machine, Larry Lewis maneuvered Quist to it. All the little man's bravado seemed to evaporate when he and Quist were alone.

"She didn't deserve it," he said, rough edges to his voice. "She and I had our problems, but she didn't deserve it."

"You think it was meant for her?" Quist asked.

"Of course not. It was meant for me," Larry said. "If I hadn't found some fun and games somewhere else, I'd be hamburger now."

"Who, Larry, and why?" Quist asked.

"The obvious is too obvious," Larry said. "Powers saw Glenda go to my cottage, thought she was there to meet me, got himself a bomb, and set it off when he thought I'd joined her there. But there are things that don't make sense about that."

"For instance?"

"That bomb had to be planned well in advance. Powers

24

could not have manufactured it on the lot when he thought I was making a play for Glenda. He wouldn't have killed Glenda knowingly, because with her old man rooting for him, she represented a small fortune in money to him. He could have been jealous, but he wouldn't have cost himself that kind of bucks. That bomb was meant for me, Julian, not Glenda, or her boyfriend, whoever he was."

"You really don't know who he was?"

Larry shook his head. "I told Shannon the truth. Glenda wanted a place where she could be alone with her friend, undiscovered by Powers. She didn't offer to tell me who her lover was, and I didn't try to get her to tell me. It happened I could do her a favor and I did it. There was no way anybody else could know in advance that I wasn't going to be in my cottage and that Glenda was. So the bomb was meant for me, set to go off when I'd surely be in bed. Whoever set it undoubtedly has a perfect alibi for the time it went off."

"It's going to make a great item for the gossip columnists," Quist said. "Man sets up a love nest for his ex-wife, who is killed by a bomb meant for him."

"She didn't deserve it," Larry said. "Her old man and Powers are the ones who should have got it. She was twenty-two years old, and Fred Forrest was still trying to run her life. He hated me. He was outraged when she accepted my invitation to the party. He wangled Powers onto the lot. She never got what she wanted; not from me, not from her father, not from anyone."

"But she was in love with you for a while. She married you."

"I've often wondered—since we split up. Did she marry me because she loved me or because she knew it would burn her old man to a crisp if she married a show-business character? But, Julian, I need your help."

"If I can."

"The place is already swarming with reporters. I can't

take a step without being surrounded by them, by friends, and somewhere an enemy—who may try again!"

"What can I do?"

"You know so many of the people, so much about them. Someone may have a notion, may have heard some gossip, may just be able to give us a lead. If you would circulate, talk, listen—"

"This is Sunday," Quist said. "There are a couple of hundred people here who have to be back on their jobs, back into their regular routines, tomorrow morning. Shannon isn't going to begin to be able to get statements from all of them. Unless he has enough evidence to make an arrest, he isn't going to be able to hold anyone here. Too many high-powered people with too much influence."

"People aren't going to talk to him anyway," Larry said. "But you—"

"There isn't going to be time to talk to many people."

"It doesn't all have to happen here," Larry said. "These people aren't going into hiding when they leave here. They can't. Most of them are too well known. The press will be on their tails. You get on to something, you could follow it up. People will talk to you because you're not a cop."

"What about you?" Quist asked. "These people are your friends."

"All but one," Larry said. "Look, I'm going to surround myself with people I can trust. The character who's out to get me may still keep coming. I don't want to be a dead hero, Julian, just a live comic!"

Quist hesitated a moment. "If I'm going to help you, Larry, you and I can't have any secrets."

"Why should we?"

"So tell me where you went after the party, where you were when the bomb exploded."

Larry's face hardened. "That's strictly private, Julian."

"It won't be for long," Quist said. "People watch every move you make, friend, because you're you. If you've been

26

having an affair with a local woman, somebody has already guessed or knows. They won't be able to resist the press, even if they don't want to talk to cops. The lady needs to be warned, told what to expect. I need to know if there's somebody in her life who might be out to get you."

Larry looked as if he didn't believe what he'd heard. He moistened his lips with the bright red tip of his tongue. "The lady has a husband," he said.

"Oh, brother!"

"But he's not here, not in town. He's away on a business trip, not expected back for another week."

"You were with this woman when the bomb went off?"

Larry nodded. "In her bed, in her house," he said. "Hell, you could have heard the bomb in the next county! Then the fire sirens! The lady called to find out where the fire was. It was a logical call for her to make. She's in local real estate. Could have been a property she was handling." Larry's mouth moved in that famous, bitter grin. "She had handled it. She was the agent through whom I bought the Inn. That's how I met her."

"So she's one of the first people Shannon will question about your local connections. Have you been in touch since you got back here and found out what had happened?"

"No chance," Larry said. "But she's probably circulating here at the Inn by now. Well known locally, logical for her to be checking on a local excitement."

"Off the top of my head, Larry," Quist said, "we have to think this was planned in advance. You were to die the night of the opening party. There would be a couple of hundred celebrities around, confusing things for the police. The bomber had to know exactly where you'd be staying, sleeping. How many of the party guests knew that? They only got here in the afternoon before the party—like me. People who knew where you'd be sleeping, living, were people on your staff, your crew, and local people who were involved in refurbishing the Inn during the couple of months beforehand. Did you make enemies here during that time—in addition to your girlfriend's husband?"

Larry shook his head. "Not that I'm aware of. I paid my bills. I didn't have any arguments with local contractors or workmen. Even the lady's husband had no reason to hate me. He hasn't been around to notice that I was interested. Believe it or not, he's a golf course architect. He's been out in the Midwest somewhere, building a new course. Just back here a couple of times since I bought the Inn and started being here."

"It's a small town," Quist said. "Someone local might let him know that you were playing games with his wife. He figures out how to get you and is gone when it happens. Only it doesn't happen."

Larry was silent for a moment. "It could be, I suppose."

"Let me talk to the lady. I won't go to Shannon with it. Let him find out for himself. But if there's any chance that it's local, we need someone who knows the people and the territory."

"I've told you enough so you can find out her name in five minutes," Larry said. "She's Madge Seaton—Mrs. Howard Seaton. Don't get her in trouble with the cops—or her husband. You do, and I'll lie my head off. She's nice, Julian. I don't want to hurt her."

Madge Seaton turned out to be just the kind of woman Quist imagined would attract Larry. She was about thirty-five, blonde, full of energy, quick laughter, not movie-star glamorous but eye-catching nonetheless. She was pointed out to Quist by the bell captain in the lobby, milling about in the crowd of celebrities waiting to be liberated by the police, reporters gunning for some juicy bit of gossip.

Quist introduced himself.

"The famous Julian Quist!" she said. "Larry told me about you. You're not going to have to do much to keep this place in the public eye, are you? It's all done for you."

28

"You say Larry told you about me," Quist said. "Was that at the party last night or later at your place?"

All the good humor vanished from the woman's face. "That miserable little jerk! He told you?"

"I'm not passing it on, I promise you, but I need your help, Madge. Can we talk somewhere?"

She started to walk away with a gesture to him to follow her. She obviously knew the Inn well, and he found himself in a card room.

"So, what's your price for silence, Quist?" she asked, as they sat down at a green-topped card table. "I knew I was a damn fool, but somehow I didn't think that Larry would—"

"He refused to tell the police where he was," Quist said. "I twisted his arm a little. I couldn't help him without knowing where the road signs pointed."

"And you think I can—or will—point?"

Quist smiled at her. "I'm lost in a strange country. And I'm not a moralist, Madge. What you and Larry do with your private lives is no concern of mine. But someone tried to murder my friend and may try again."

"Is it certain it was Glenda Forrest and some guy of hers?"

"No medical identification of Glenda, but Larry loaned her the cottage. Who else? When the police find some man is missing, they'll be able to make a guess about her companion. But I'm scratching an itch that tells me the bomber could have been somebody local."

Madge's eyes widened. "Local?"

"Like your husband "

She threw back her head and laughed. "Howie? You're off your rocker, Quist! Howie's in Ohio. Why would he want to—?"

"If you were my woman," Quist said, "and you were playing around with someone else, I might just hate the guy enough to let him have it."

"Am I supposed to take that as a compliment?" Madge

29

asked. Her smile came back. "Well, I will—and thanks."

"Only local people who worked on fixing up the Inn and members of Larry's staff would know where he was quartered and where to set up a bomb in advance. You've had two months here in town to hear anyone bad-mouth him. I don't know how long you and Larry have been having a thing, but probably long enough for some local busybody to get word to your husband. The killer couldn't guess that on the party night Larry would lend his cottage to someone else."

"If someone tipped Howie off, would he plan to bomb a place where he'd have to guess I might be?" Madge asked.

"He might. I don't know him, so I can't answer that."

"It's all crazy as hell," Madge said. She sat silent for a moment, frowning over what she was thinking. "Yes," she said, finally, "Larry and I have been having 'a thing,' as you call it, for about a month. Howie has been building a new golf course in Ohio. He's only been back a couple of times in the last two months. He has a private plane. He flies back for a night and goes again."

"Was he here yesterday or the day before?"

"No!"

"Not that you know of."

"He couldn't come back here without my knowing. Too many people would know he'd flown in his plane." She leaned forward, gripping the edge of the card table. "Let me tell you about Howie and me." She took a deep breath. "We were high school sweethearts. Like most kids do these days, we went the whole way back then. I got pregnant. We decided to make it legal, and we got married. That's seventeen years ago. I—I lost the baby, and I can't ever have children." Her grip tightened on the table.

"I'm sorry," Quist said.

"I went into the real estate business with my mother. My father died years ago. I became a high-powered busi-

30

nesswoman. Howie was golf-crazy and he finally hit it big when he redesigned the course here in town. He got jobs all over the country, most of them places far away from here. I could have traveled with him, I suppose, but I had my business here and it was profitable. Rich people were buying into the area. I—I found I had problems."

"Sexual problems?"

She nodded. "I'm not a potential mother anymore, so there are no risks involved in casual sex. Howie was gone for long stretches of time. I love him, you understand? He's my guy. But—but I can't help responding to physical excitement. I've never had an affair with any commitments involved. Just for fun! I thought I played it pretty cool. I never let myself be tangled up in a romance. I never played it so that it would get back to Howie and hurt him."

"It's pretty hard to be private about an affair with Larry Lewis. He isn't the private type," Quist said.

"It wasn't so hard," Madge said. "I had business dealings with him. I sold him the Inn. I sold him surrounding property. I found local contractors to do the work for him. I found local people to staff the place. It was natural for us to be seen around together. And I—well, I grew up on his films. It's strange, but you feel as though you know famous actors even though you don't know them. When he made a pass at me, there was a kind of extra excitement to it because he was a star. I guess I knew he'd be fun in bed. He'd had all those famous women! And he was! He is! He never asked for anything but the moment at hand. When Howie came home, Larry was just a business associate. He never pretended to be anything else. Howie thinks he's a great guy, good fun. He doesn't dream that there's anything between Larry and me but business."

"But you took him home to your place last night."

"The first and only time he ever came to Howie's house," Madge said. "He just wanted to get away from the report-

31

ers, the famous people. Believe it or not, he just slept in the next room. He was pooped out. It was the one time like that that we didn't have fun together."

"Larry may need you for an alibi," Quist said.

"Alibi for what?" She seemed genuinely surprised.

"The police may think he meant to kill Glenda," Quist said. "Killed her because she turned him down for somebody else. Set her up in the cottage and murdered her and her lover."

"How crazy can they be?" Madge said, laughing again. "Well, if he needs an alibi I'll supply him with one. I'll tell the truth. He wanted to get away from the Inn, the reporters, the fans. I offered him a bed in my house and he accepted it."

"He says he was in your bed, in your house."

"All the beds in my house are my beds," she said. "I've told you the truth, Julian."

"Will anyone believe it?"

"Will it matter, as long as Howie believes it?"

The door to the card room opened and a dark-haired, attractive-looking man came in.

"Darling! I've been looking all over hell for you," the man said, and headed for Madge, holding out his hands. She stood up to greet him, turning to Quist.

"This is my husband, Howie Seaton—Julian Quist."

"I found I could get away for a couple of days last night," Seaton said. "I tried to call you, but I suppose you were at the party, so I just took off. It seems like all hell broke loose here. I didn't know a thing about it till I landed at the town airport. You're all right?"

"I'm fine," Madge said. She glanced at Quist. "But there's something I have to tell you."

"Tell away," Seaton said. He had his arm around his wife, smiling down at her.

"You have no idea what a madhouse it was here last night," Madge said to her husband. "I mean at the party.

32

As it was breaking up, Larry Lewis complained that he wasn't going to be able to get any sleep—reporters, fans. I told him there was a bed in our house he could use and he accepted. He was there when the bomb exploded. Quist was here to tell me that Larry may have to tell the police where he was. Now the whole town will be suggesting that Larry was sleeping with me."

Seaton bent down and kissed his wife's cheek. "Well, as long as you weren't," he said. Either he loved his wife and trusted her completely, or he was the greatest actor Quist had even seen.

3

Things were quieter in the Inn's lobby when Quist left the Seatons and went out to find Larry. Larry needed to be told what Madge Seaton's story was going to be. Bobby Crown was at the desk and signaled to Quist.

"Looking for you. Didn't know where you were," Bobby said.

"Things seem to be thinning out," Quist said.

"People leaving as fast as the cops will clear them. No traffic here because there are no checkouts. Everybody was Larry's guest. But we have some new arrivals—Fred Forrest and a small army of his, including his own private eye."

"The cops know it was Glenda?" Quist asked.

"Still only Larry's story," Bobby said. "But no one doubts it. Forrest is blowing up a storm. He isn't going to leave it to 'hick cops' to nail his daughter's killer."

"Rough for him."

"I was looking for you because Forrest wants to talk to

you. He's taken over a private dining room at the rear there."

"What does he want with me?" Quist asked.

"You're Larry's public relations man. Forrest wants to tell you what you can and cannot tell the press."

"Wants to protect his daughter's 'fair name'?"

"I suppose," Bobby said.

The scene in the private dining room was certainly not a happy holiday gathering. You saw no one when you first walked in except Frederick Forrest, iron-gray hair, pale eyes, mouth a grim slit. He was, Quist thought, the perfect prototype of the powerful business tycoon. Three young men in dark business suits, a girl secretary sitting at a stenotype machine, and a rough-looking character standing a little distance who was, Quist guessed, the private detective. It was a scene right out of a film.

"You're Julian Quist?" Forrest's voice was husky, harsh.

Quist nodded. "I don't quite know why I'm here, Mr. Forrest. I don't like being 'summoned.'"

"I couldn't care less what you like, Quist. You're here to get orders."

"I'll listen, but I'll only perform if I like what I hear," Quist said.

"You'll do what you're told, Quist."

Quist turned and started for the door. The man he'd decided was the private eye blocked his way.

"Don't try to smart-alec it, man," he said.

Quist looked back at Forrest. "This is the second time one of your goons has threatened to get physical with me." The three young men in the dark suits had drifted around to back up the detective.

"I want you to listen to what I have to say to you," Forrest said. "It's up to you how difficult you make it."

"I'll listen," Quist said. "I'll also decide what to do about what I hear." He reminded himself that this man's daughter

34

had been blown to pieces, burned to ashes. The fierce anger he must feel shouldn't be held against him.

"It's partly because you are Shorty Lewis's public relations man, and partly because I know you by reputation that I want you to listen," Forrest said.

"So I'm listening."

"Perhaps you can guess how I must have felt when I was wakened at daybreak in my townhouse in New York and told that my daughter had been murdered."

"That's *why* I'm listening," Quist said.

"I had a premonition about the party that miserable little bastard Lewis was planning. I was sickened by all the publicity about Lewis's four ex-wives attending. I did everything I could to persuade Glenda not to come, not to collaborate with a vulgarity."

"You apparently weren't persuasive enough."

"Glenda is—was, God help me—twenty-two years old. I could cut off her funds, take away her car, cancel her charge accounts and credit cards. But short of hog-tying her and locking her in the basement, there was no way of stopping her."

"So you sent your man Powers along to watchdog her," Quist said.

"Not only Powers," Forrest said. "I also sent a man named Pat McNally to act as her chauffeur and to be on hand in case she needed help of any kind."

"Why would she have needed help?"

"Anyone who's involved with that miserable little bastard she married could need help," Forrest said. His hatred was so intense, his voice almost sizzled. "I don't know for sure yet, but we think the other body they found in the cottage was McNally's."

Quist's eyes widened. "She was having an affair with the chauffeur?"

"Damn you!" Forrest said. He took a step toward Quist,

fists clenched. Then he backed away. "It's just that kind of story that I want squelched. McNally hasn't shown up. My guess is that after the bomb went off, Pat tried to get into the cottage to rescue Glenda and paid for it with his life."

"According to Larry Lewis—"

"That forked-tongued little monster! Glenda wanted the cottage to entertain a lover, hide away from Paul Powers? Lewis has to have some kind of story to cover up his own actions. If Glenda was having an affair, she wouldn't share that information with Lewis."

"Why not? They were friends, he had the accommodations to please her."

"More likely he wanted to get even with her for running out on their marriage after less than a year. That made him look like the punk he is."

"Are you suggesting," Quist asked, "that he threw a bomb into his own cottage to kill your daughter?"

"It's certainly an avenue to explore," Forrest said.

"Larry was somewhere else, away from the Inn," Quist said.

"He says!"

The detective character spoke for the first time. "My name is Ben Ryan, Quist, private investigator working on the case for Mr. Forrest. It wouldn't change things if Lewis can prove he was somewhere else. If there was a timer on the bomb, that's just the way he would stage it, wouldn't he?"

Quist didn't answer. Larry could prove that he wasn't on the lot when the bomb was exploded if he had to. Madge Seaton was ready, even if what she had to tell wasn't quite the whole truth. When no one else spoke, Quist tried a new tack.

"Listening to your theories is fascinating, Mr. Forrest, but it isn't what I should be doing at the moment. Reporters from all the media are waiting for some kind of statement. I've got to be ready to handle Larry's end of it when the time comes. So, if you'll excuse me—"

"You're here to be told what to tell the media," Forrest said.

"Make it quick," Quist said.

"Lewis's story that Glenda asked for a place where she could entertain a lover without Paul Powers knowing has to be buried," Forrest said.

"But if it's the truth?"

"It's not the truth, and if Lewis persists in it, you can tell him for me I'll arrange to have his tongue cut out!"

"With me as a witness to the threat?"

"I can and will pulverize Julian Quist Associates if I have to," Forrest said.

Quist's smile was wry. "You've given me just about the best story for the press they could dream of," he said. "Your daughter's affair with the chauffeur must be kept under cover. If it isn't, you'll cut out Larry Lewis's tongue and destroy Julian Quist Associates. You're not very expert at throwing your weight around, Forrest. You'd better have your denials polished up because I may decide to tell the press just that."

As he turned to go, Quist found himself chest-to-chest with Ben Ryan, the private eye.

"You'd better give that some careful thought, Quist," the detective said. "If you don't, you may suddenly find you've become accident-prone."

Threats were not exactly the way to win friends and influence people in Quist's case. Forrest was a powerhouse who undoubtedly had the machinery for destroying people, but bombastic threats seemed somehow out of character. You had to remember, Quist told himself, that what had happened to Forrest was beyond anything the man could have been ready to face. Less than twenty-four hours ago he had argued with Glenda, alive, beautiful, spirited. He had anticipated some kind of dirty trick from Larry Lewis, but he couldn't have imagined his daughter's total physical destruction. He couldn't have imagined that the next time he saw her she would be ashes in a jug in the medical examiner's lab. Forrest, hearing the news, had rushed to the scene with his little army, ready to do battle with a killer, but so far there was no real evidence to point to anyone. He could only swing at the wind. Melodramatic threats could be a way to let off steam that might otherwise destroy him.

If Forrest deserved an excuse that might be it, but Quist was more concerned with finding Larry Lewis to tell him of his encounter with the Seatons. People were still moving out through the lobby to waiting cars. All these merrymakers of yesterday wanted now was to get back to their normal surroundings as quickly as possible—with a gory story with which to entertain their friends for months.

Bobby Crown, looking about as exhausted as a man can be, was at the front desk when Quist asked where he might find Larry Lewis.

"He may be in my room," Bobby said, "looking for something to wear. Everything personal that he owned, right down to his toothbrush, was destroyed in the cottage. Shannon has ordered him not to leave the Inn. That goes for the three ex-wives, me, the staff, you. I am supposed to tell you that."

"What about Powers and Forrest and his gang?"

"They'll have to leave over the bodies of some dead state troopers," Bobby said. "Anyone with any connection to Glenda is, you might say, under house arrest."

"Has Forrest reported on his other man who was here, the chauffeur, McNally?"

"At the top of his lungs," Bobby said. "He had a bed in the servants' quarters, but we haven't found him."

"Could he have been the man in the cottage? Forrest

thinks he might have tried to rescue Glenda after the bomb exploded."

"Your guess is as good as mine," Bobby said. "We haven't found him. Nor have we been able to turn up some other man who was at the party who is missing this morning."

"Where is your room? I want to talk to Larry."

"Third floor, room number two," Bobby said. "He may just be staying out of sight up there. Everybody wants to say good-bye, and how sorry they are, and all that crap."

Larry wasn't in Bobby's room on the third floor, but there was evidence that he'd been there. Three or four suits and jackets had been taken out of the closet and left draped over the bed; a collection of shirts had been removed from the bureau, as though Larry had been trying to make a selection. But he wasn't there now.

There was a knock on the door, but before Quist could answer it was opened by Captain Shannon's trooper.

"Where is he?" the trooper asked.

"Bobby? He's down at the front desk as far as I know."

"I'm not talking about Crown, I'm talking about Lewis," the trooper said. He crossed the room and opened the bathroom door. "If that character has walked out on us, he isn't going to know what hit him. I was also looking for you, Quist. Andrew Martin, the county attorney, is here and he wants to talk to you—down where Shannon is."

Andrew Martin was a not unattractive man in his late thirties, about Quist's age. He was the first person Quist had seen for some hours who didn't look disturbed or angry. He greeted Quist with a friendly smile.

"I know quite a lot about you secondhand, Mr. Quist," he said. "Your business partner, Dan Garvey, is an old friend of mine. We went to the same college, played on the same football team. I've just finished talking to him on the phone. You get a top rating from him."

"Nice to hear," Quist said.

"I've seen Dan a few times in the last couple of months,

here in town. He was handling Larry Lewis's public relations. I expected to find him here, but I was told you'd taken his place."

"Dan was also handling the heavyweight boxing championship. When the fight was delayed, he couldn't be two places at once." Quist shook his head. "Would you believe I don't even know how the fight came out."

"The champ held on to his title," Martin said. "Technical knockout in two minutes of the fifth round. But you had Lewis's ear for the last day. Shannon tells me you were present when Lewis was threatened by a man named Powers who was one of Forrest's people."

"Glenda Forrest was also present," Quist said.

"Unfortunately she can't tell us about it. Now Lewis has taken a powder on us."

"You think he's left the Inn?"

"Unless he's hiding someplace we haven't discovered yet. Most likely he's gone somewhere to buy himself some new clothes. He isn't a man who's inclined to obey orders if he wants to do something else, I suspect." Martin glanced across the room to where Captain Shannon was talking to a man Quist recognized as the maître d' at last night's party. "Shannon isn't pleased. He's got troopers out combing the town for Lewis."

"He can't go anywhere without being recognized," Quist said. "The whole world knows him by sight. You should have him back any minute."

"I suspect you can help us while we wait," Martin said.

"I'm not sure I know how," Quist said.

"You talked to him this morning—in the next office," Martin said. "Did he tell you more than he told Shannon? Like where he went after the party—a lady somewhere?"

There was no reason not to tell what he knew now. "He went to the home of a Mrs. Seaton, the real estate agent who handled his property deal here."

"Howie Seaton isn't going to like that when he hears it," Martin said.

"He's heard it and he's not distressed," Quist said. "Larry just wanted to get away from the mob here, and she offered him a guest room at her house. Seaton turned up this morning, knows, and sees nothing out of line about it."

"You think that's the way it was?"

"I'm tell you what I was told by Mrs. Seaton, in her husband's presence. Seaton didn't seem to have any reason not to trust his wife."

"Why didn't Lewis want to tell that to Captain Shannon?"

"Perhaps, because of his reputation, he was afraid people wouldn't believe his stay there at the Seaton house wasn't just a way to avoid the press and his fans. It would make for gossip that would hurt Madge Seaton and her husband."

"Which, of course, it will as soon as it becomes public."

"Perhaps you can keep it quiet when you've checked it out," Quist said. "I haven't told anyone until now."

"Perhaps we can, if Howie Seaton has an alibi for himself," Martin said. "Does Lewis think the bomb was meant for him?"

"He has no doubt of it."

"Did he suggest to you who might have it in for him?"

"No. But nobody knew he wasn't going to be in the cottage and Glenda was. He believes the bomb had to be meant for him, planned in advance, before any arrangement was made for Glenda to have the use of the cottage."

"Forrest thinks Lewis may have set the bomb himself because he had it in for his ex-wife—Forrest's daughter," Martin said.

"I've just come from seeing Forrest," Quist said. "He wants it any way except the way Larry tells it—that she wanted to duck Powers so she could shack up with someone else."

"And there was someone," Martin said, his good humor fading.

"Forrest says it was his chauffeur, trying to rescue her."

"I know," Martin said. "And we haven't found the chauffeur, so it could be. But that still doesn't lead us to who set the bomb intended for Lewis. Did you know Glenda Forrest?"

"No," Quist said. "I'd seen her around in the city with Larry, but I never actually met her until yesterday afternoon in the cottage. I assume she'd been arranging with Larry to take over the cottage when I turned up. Then there was Powers, shouting threats, and Glenda took off."

"Did she and Lewis seem friendly before Powers arrived?"

"Old and good friends," Quist said.

"You heard anything that might make you believe she was involved with a lover she was trying to hide from her old man?"

"In my world, Martin, famous people are always suspected of having free and easy love lives. People want to think it, so they think it and say it. Glenda was married to Larry, which is a juicy piece of gossip in itself, suggesting an affair beforehand. The marriage lasted for less than a year, so there was probably talk about both of them playing around. What you believe is what you want to believe, I guess."

"Can you suggest anyone who might have any reliable facts about Glenda?"

Quist hesitated. "There are three other ex-wives here at the Inn," he said. "It's possible that one or all of them may have had a special interest in Larry's goings-on, in Glenda, who was their most recent replacement."

"You know any of them personally?"

"I know Sandra Ames, who was number one, quite well. She was a client at one time. I know the others to say hello to, but not much better than that."

"Would you be willing to sit in while we ask Miss Ames what she can tell us about Glenda? It might make it easier for her if someone she knows is present."

"My job is to help with the press, which is clamoring for information," Quist said.

"We're not giving anything out until we have some solid facts, Quist. We still have to make an official identification of the dead people, although we're sure the woman is Glenda Forrest. In the meantime, if you'd be willing to help with Miss Ames—?"

While Martin set out to find Sandra Ames, Quist waited in the office, juggling an array of speculations. Captain Shannon had finished with the maître d' and taken off, presumably to intensify the search for Larry. As he was leaving the room, Shannon stopped to ask Quist if Larry had said anything to him that might suggest where he'd gone. Quist had nothing for him.

The maître d' wandered over to Quist. They were alone in the office for the moment. The man was tall, dark, with a carefully cultivated air of elegance.

"I know you, Mr. Quist," the man said. "Larry pointed you out to me last night during the party. If I had any problems with the press, I was to call on you. My name is Juan Ricardo. It's hard to believe such a gay evening could turn into horror."

Ricardo was, Quist thought, more like a Spanish nobleman than a headwaiter. "You've known Larry for a long time?" Quist asked him.

"Many years," Ricardo said. "But I only started working for him a few weeks ago when we were preparing to open Rainbow Hill. I had been the maître d' at the Club Madrid in New York. It has been one of Larry Lewis's favorite hangouts—after theater pleasures—ever since I can remember. In my business, you remember handsome tippers and try to make them happy. When Mr. Lewis planned to

43

open this place, he made me an offer I couldn't turn down. The Club Madrid has changed owners recently, so there was no matter of loyalty involved."

"Most of us think the bomb was meant for Larry," Quist said. "Do you know or have you heard of anyone who might have wanted to destroy Larry?"

Ricardo shook his head. "The trooper captain has just been asking me that. I've only known Larry over the years as a patron of the Madrid and for the last six weeks as my new employer. I haven't known his personal life at all, except that there has been a parade of beautiful ladies he brought to the Madrid over the years. You learn to assume gossip, which I get to hear in my position, is false most of the time."

"Were there public quarrels?"

"Never," Ricardo said. "He is one of the best liked, I might even say best loved, of all the big stars I've encountered over the years. If friendship is wealth, he's a rich man."

"You knew Glenda Forrest, his fourth wife?"

Ricardo nodded, slowly. "Poor girl. They say there isn't enough left of her to recognize. Yes, I knew her. Believe it or not, Larry met her in the Club Madrid. There were periods of time when we didn't see Larry at the Club. He'd be on the Coast, months at a time, making a film. In one of those periods Miss Forrest became a regular customer of the Club's. She came three or four nights a week, with a whole collection of different men. She was very lovely, very bright and gay; people watched her and envied the men who brought her."

"No regular beau?"

"I think not. Oh, there were three or four repeaters, but they didn't repeat more than once—twice at the most."

"You knew she stood to inherit the Forrest oil millions? Did it surprise you that one man wasn't hanging on to her for dear life?"

"I think the lady controlled her own life—except for her father," Ricardo said.

"You know him?"

"Not with pleasure," Ricardo said, his face darkening. Then he smiled. "He was raising hell at the Club one night, trying to get his daughter away from some young man she was dating. Papa had a couple of goons with him, and Glenda's young man wasn't backing off. I thought we were about to have a brawl. Suddenly the orchestra struck up and the customers began to applaud—not the Forrest brawl but Larry, who was suddenly on the stage doing one of his remarkable dances. I hadn't seen him for months. People were shushing Forrest and his goons, and suddenly Glenda had an army on her side—an army that wanted to watch Larry undisturbed. The manager had called the cops and while Larry danced, Forrest, his goons, and Glenda's young man were quietly ejected. Larry finished his dance and came down off the stage to Glenda's table. 'I'm not husky enough to handle those characters,' he said, 'but I thought I might create a distraction.' He turned to me. 'Champagne for the lady, Ricardo,' he said." Ricardo's smile widened. "Two weeks later they were married!"

"Forrest has it in for Larry, but he wasn't here last night," Quist said.

"He wouldn't have to be," Ricardo said. "He can hire all the killers he needs. He had two men here, didn't he, watching her? Powers and this missing chauffeur he says may have been the man in the cottage, killed on a rescue mission? He could have planned to knock Larry off, the wires got crossed, and his own daughter was in the cottage."

"What about people who worked for Larry?" Quist asked. "Some nut who had a grudge against him for something?"

"I wouldn't know, but I'd bet my life against it," Ricardo said. "I've only worked for him for about six weeks, but

45

others, like Bobby Crown, have worked for him for years and would let a steamroller run over them if Larry asked them to. I was in charge of the party last night. 'It's your ballgame,' he told me. Not a word of criticism or negative advice. If I'd made a blunder, he'd have stood behind me. Working for a man like Larry is everyone's dream."

"Seeing him dead was someone's dream," Quist said.

Andrew Martin came back into the office, escorting Sandra Ames. Ricardo bowed to the lady.

"Miss Ames," he said. "It's not easy to find anything to be grateful for in a horror situation like this, but thank God the person we both care for is safe."

"Let's hope he is," Martin said; his relaxed manner had grown grim. He turned to Quist. "We can't find Lewis."

"Can't find him?"

"He seems to have disappeared," Martin said.

"He was up in Bobby Crown's room looking for some clothes to borrow," Quist said.

"I know. But Crown has just been up there and he says Larry didn't take anything."

"So he's gone somewhere else for clothes; into town, somewhere to buy what he needs for the moment."

"He has two cars here," Martin said. "A white Mercedes and a yellow Toyota. They're both in the garage where they belong. It begins to look as if he's taken a powder on us for some reason."

"What reason?"

"You've got me," Martin said. "He may have decided he'd be safer somewhere else. But why he'd go without telling Captain Shannon, who could protect him, or Bobby Crown, who is his closest associate, I can't imagine."

"He told me he was going to gather friends and people he could trust around him and stay put," Quist said. "He said something about preferring to be a live comic to a dead hero."

"Larry can't go twenty yards anywhere in the world,

openly, without being recognized," Sandra Ames said. "He couldn't walk away from here in broad daylight without being seen. He can't pass himself off as anyone but Larry Lewis, even wearing a Halloween false face."

"Forgive me for butting in," Ricardo said, "but the fact that he hasn't told anyone he was going somewhere suggests to me that he hasn't gone."

"They've scoured the Inn from cellar to attic," Martin said. "Nobody's seen him since he went up to Crown's room to find some clothes."

"I think he was there," Quist said. "He'd taken out some suits, jackets, shirts to make a choice. I assumed he'd found something and just not bothered to put things back."

"This building—the Inn—is just a small part of Larry's property here," Ricardo said. "There's a clubhouse down at the golf course. He could have had a locker there with clothes in it. There are stables and bathhouses down by the pool. He could be in any number of places where you haven't looked."

"He could also have just slipped away with someone who was leaving," Martin said. "Dozens of his friends have been heading out when Shannon cleared them. He could have gone out in the back of someone's car and never been seen at all."

"Does it occur to you," Quist said, after a moment of silence, "that he could have been taken away against his will by someone who missed killing him with that bomb and is going to try another way now?"

"Oh God," Sandra Ames said.

PART
TWO

1

The projected interview with Sandra Ames was delayed while Shannon and his troopers and most of the Inn's staff involved themselves in an almost inch-by-inch search of the Rainbow Hill property for Larry Lewis. At a little past noon Shannon and Andrew Martin, the county attorney, came to the reluctant conclusion that Larry was gone, willingly or unwillingly. He was nowhere: not in any of the outbuildings. Deputies were still searching the woods to the north of the Inn. The marble swimming pool had been drained, although that hadn't really been necessary as the water in it was clear as window glass. It didn't make sense that Larry could be strolling around the ski trails or bridle paths—not willingly. But they were being searched.

Bobby Crown, obviously tortured by anxiety for his long-time friend and employer, wasn't able to suggest any place Larry might have chosen to go by himself. He repeated that Larry hadn't taken any clothes from his room, but he might have been interrupted while he was trying to make a choice and had left the room—willingly or unwillingly. That seemed to be the name of the feeling, willingly or unwillingly, and more and more Quist's theory was being adopted by everyone. Larry had left Rainbow Hill unwillingly.

"I have to believe what I suggested earlier," Martin said. "He left in a car with people who had been cleared by Shannon to go, quite probably, I tend to think now, against his will."

"But wouldn't he have been seen in a car?" Sandra Ames

asked. She hadn't left the office since she'd first been brought there almost two hours before. Answers were too important to her for her not to be present if there were to be any answers.

"Not if he was bound and gagged, hidden under a robe or locked in a truck," Martin said.

"It's just not believable," Sandra said.

"I asked you to come here originally, Miss Ames, with the hope that you could give us a lead to someone who could hate Larry Lewis so fiercely. If what we're beginning to believe is true and Lewis was taken away against his will, that person had to be here, probably at the party last night, later when the bomb was set off, and this morning when Larry was taken away from here, dead or alive. Can you help us? You've known Lewis for a long time, known his friends, the details of his career, heard all the gossip that's involved him in that time. Can you give us just one hint that would point us in the right direction?"

Nobody knew better than Quist how skillful this woman was as an actress. Camera! Action! She was about to play a scene, he thought. Was that shaken voice real or part of a performance? Was that still-lovely face, moving with emotion, genuine or part of a script she was writing for herself as she went along? Quist found himself believing what he saw and heard and yet knowing that she had the skill to make him react exactly as she wanted. Martin, not familiar with stage and film talents, would surely be taken in by her if it was phony.

"It is a long time," Sandra said. "Forty years ago last month Larry and I were married. I was eighteen, Larry was twenty-three." She gave Martin a tiny little smile. "You are the first person I've told my right age to in a great many years, Mr. Martin."

"I wouldn't believe it if I didn't know some of Larry Lewis's history," Martin said.

"Thank you, sir," Sandra said, and the polite games were

over. "I should think Bobby Crown would be the person who knows the most about Larry's life for the last twenty-five or thirty years. He's been involved with Larry every day for at least that long."

"He's drawn a blank so far," Martin said. "Everybody we've talked to comes up with the same answer, Miss Ames. Larry Lewis is a spectacular star, the nicest, kindest, most generous guy in the world. He has nothing but friends and well-wishers everywhere. And yet, Miss Ames, you are one of four women who couldn't make it with him."

"Are you suggesting that I—?"

"I'm suggesting that you, who couldn't make it with him after five years of marriage, are still his friend, which backs up the Mr. Wonderful theory. But he isn't Mr. Wonderful to someone, Miss Ames."

"To try to kill him so violently—" Sandra said in that unsteady voice.

"When you've been dealing with crime as long as I have, Miss Ames, you discover that the motive for violence doesn't have to be earthshaking. A sick mind takes over and turns something that seems insignificant into hate. An unintended slight, an imagined insult, professional or personal jealousy can grow and fester and lead to a payoff long, long after whatever it was that happened. It is that kind of sickness that we have to look for, and you, who have known Larry for so very long, might remember some small event in his past—a molehill that has grown into a mountain."

Sandra shook her head slowly. "Larry and I separated and were divorced thirty-five years ago. The five years that we were together I wouldn't trade for anything."

"Mr. Wonderful!" Martin said.

"It started wonderfully," Sandra said. "Larry had taken his first step toward the top, a film. I had a bit part in that movie, and I was fascinated with the way that little ugly young man could turn himself into something romantic. It had to be acting, I thought. He couldn't *be* romantic for

53

real. And then—then I was swept off my feet—a passionate affair, and then marriage. The most important thing about those next five years is that they were fun! He was fun to be with. I didn't discover any dark side to that lively man. He was climbing a tricky ladder—the show-business ladder. It was my world, too, and there were people I thought were unfair, or incompetent, ready to walk over me if they thought it would help them. I hated those people. Larry was different. He just laughed when someone tried to get in his way, played some kind of a dirty trick on him. He would act more effectively, sing better, dance more brilliantly, keep climbing to the top and to hell with them. He never tried to get back at anybody, to get even. He just kept climbing until he got where he is now, at the very top."

"I'm not looking for someone he hated, Miss Ames. I'm after someone who hates him."

"If you can just hate a man for being the best at what he does, then I suppose there could be hundreds," Sandra said. "Envy, jealousy, perhaps, but hate? You have to hurt somebody for them to hate you. I've never known of anyone that Larry deliberately hurt, and there are so many that he helped—like me, like Bev, like Patti."

"His other wives?" Martin asked.

"Yes."

"But your marriage broke up, and the others, too," Martin said.

"I don't know if I can explain it to you, Mr. Martin." She glanced at Quist. "Maybe Julian will understand. It took me a while to come up with the answer for myself. I think for Larry marriage is like a long-run play. You open in it, you get marvelous notices, and you play it for months, maybe years. After a while the excitement wears off. You are doing the same thing over and over. The play is just as good, you are just as good, but it isn't a challenge anymore. You want a new play, a new opening, new notices, and a new success. I think that's the way it is with Larry. Everything is fine, but after a while you need a new vehicle. Larry and I were separated by different films we were working in and—well, it just came to an end. No quarrels, no bitterness, but it was time to close the show."

"That's how it was with the others?" Martin asked.

"With Bev and Patti, I think so. I knew them both professionally. It isn't surprising, is it, that over the years we compared notes? The show had its run, was a success, but after a while Larry had to find a new challenge. Five years seemed to be about as long as he could play one script."

"He was married to Glenda for less than a year," Quist said.

Sandra smiled. "The play didn't get good notices. It didn't run. Glenda wanted him to stop being a performer and become a rancher. It was a part he couldn't play."

"Why does Fred Forrest hate him so much?" Quist asked.

"He didn't want Larry to marry her in the first place, and he hated him for staying friends with her after they separated."

Martin made an impatient gesture. "We're not getting anywhere, Miss Ames," he said. "You were a guest of honor at the party last night. You must have known almost everyone present through your own career and Lewis's. Someone who had it in for him? Someone who hated him?"

"Last night wasn't like a public performance to which anyone could buy tickets," Sandra said. "You were there by Larry's invitation only. It doesn't seem likely he'd invite enemies."

"But some friend could bring a friend who was not in love with Lewis," Martin said.

"I don't think so," Sandra said. "I know I was asked if there was someone I thought he'd overlooked. I couldn't think of anyone offhand when I saw the guest list. 'I know there are people you might like to have with you,' Larry told me, 'but the Inn can accommodate only so many people, and my personal friends come first.'"

"There was Paul Powers," Quist said.

Sandra nodded. "I know, but it was rather a special situation. Forrest threatened to keep Glenda from coming, if necessary by force, unless Powers was here to protect her."

"Protect her from what?"

"From Larry!" Sandra's smile was forced. "Larry was tempted to tell the whole Forrest gang to drop dead, but he wanted Glenda here. A man who is friends with all his ex-wives was an image he wanted to present."

"And that image was real, not a fake?" Martin asked. "The ex-wives are his friends?"

"Good friends," Sandra said.

"So there was no one at the party you thought of as an enemy? No stranger you might suspect just because he was a stranger?"

"No one," Sandra said.

"This seems to be a dead end," Martin said, his face clouded. "But let me ask you one more question, Miss Ames. Can you guess who the man was with whom Glenda wanted to spend the night in Lewis's cottage?"

Sandra shook her head. "If you were to ask me who Bev or Patti might want as a lover I might make a guess, but not Glenda. She didn't move in our world, the show-business world. The gossip columnists weren't always watching her for a story. She and I were friendly, but not the kind of close friends who share intimate secrets. I suppose she told Larry."

"If he knows he wouldn't tell us when we first asked, and now we can't find him to ask again."

"But the man is dead—isn't he?" Sandra asked.

"If he is, who was he? Forrest tried to tell us there was no lover; that the man who died in the bombing was his chauffeur who was trying to effect a rescue."

"If it was the chauffeur," Quist said in a flat voice, "then the lover is walking around, free and clear, and keeping just as far away from this whole mess as he can. We need to find out who he was—or is."

Martin gave Quist a sour little smile. "Be my guest," he said.

Fred Forrest had done everything he could to prevent the story that his daughter had died in the bombing with a lover from making headlines. The dead man in the cottage was McNally, her chauffeur and bodyguard, who had failed in a rescue attempt. The three young men in the dark suits circulated among the reporters from the press, television, and radio, hinting that the wrong story could lead to staggering libel suits.

Dick Reeves, anchorman for one of the major TV network news teams, was an old friend of Quist's. He was lying in wait when Quist emerged from the Inn's office with Sandra Ames.

"No more mouth-shut, baby," he said. He said hello to Sandra. He obviously knew her, too. "Where's your boy, Julian?"

"If you mean Larry, I wish I knew," Quist said.

"No question that the dead woman in the cottage is Glenda Forrest, wife number four?"

"There hasn't been an official identification, Dick, but there's no doubt about it. They have Larry's testimony before he disappeared, and Forrest doesn't deny it. After all, he can't produce her alive."

"And the man with her—?"

"Either a lover, or a bodyguard on a rescue mission. Too little left of him to be quickly identified."

"So the lover comes forward or the chauffeur-bodyguard comes forward and we know," Reeves said.

"If it's the chauffeur, McNally, the lover won't come forward, because he doesn't want to involve himself or hurt

57

Glenda's reputation. If it's the lover, McNally won't come forward because Forrest may have McNally on the way to the South Pole by now."

"Is there any question the bomb was meant for Larry?" Reeves asked.

"Not in my mind," Quist said.

"So why are we worried about lovers and bodyguards if it wasn't meant for them?"

"Personally, I'm not concerned about them," Quist said. "I don't see how discovering whether it's a lover or McNally who died in the cottage will help to point to the person who set the bomb and who may already have taken his second shot at Larry."

"So what direction are you headed in?" Reeves asked.

Quist shook his head. "Circles," he said. "So far I can't make any kind of guess."

"I'll play ball with you if you'll play ball with us," Reeves said.

Any kind of help, especially from the network reporters, would be welcome. "A deal," Quist said. He glanced over at the front desk. Bobby Crown was there, staring straight ahead of him at nothing, like a man in a trance. Quist left Reeves and Sandra and walked over to Larry's little business manager. "Could we talk for a few minutes, Bobby?"

Bobby turned his head and his eyes looked glazed. "Everybody has," he said. "Troopers, county attorney, every damn guest who was here for the party. Why not you, Quist?"

"Can we go somewhere we won't be interrupted?"

"Why not? Forrest and his gang have evacuated the private dining room."

No one had cleaned up the private dining room. Ash trays were full, and there was the aroma of expensive cigars. Nothing but the best for Fred Forrest. Bobby sat down at the table in the center of the room and covered his face with his hands. "Up all day yesterday preparing for the party," he said. "Then the party, got to bed a little after five. An hour and a half sleep, and then this hell broke loose!"

"We're all in pretty much the same boat," Quist said.

"Not so," Bobby said. "I'm supposed to know everything."

"What do you know that I don't know?" Quist asked.

"One thing that nobody else seems to be saying," Bobby said. "The story Forrest is trying to sell just won't wash. McNally, the chauffeur-bodyguard guy, was never killed trying to rescue Glenda. If he was outside, watching the cottage when the bomb went off, he never in God's world would have tried to go in after Glenda. In ten seconds the whole place was totaled. Not even the hero of heroes would have rushed in—could have—the flames were so intense."

"So where is he? He hasn't checked in with the troopers."

"I didn't say he wasn't in the cottage," Bobby said. "I said he wasn't there on a rescue mission."

"You're suggesting Glenda was having an affair with her chauffeur?"

Bobby shrugged. "Why not? He was a man, an attractive-looking guy. His job was to be around Glenda night and day. I'm guessing that's the way it was. They were in the hay together, laughing at her father, when the bomb went off."

"Could be," Quist said.

"Forrest will spend a fortune to prevent us from making it stick—if he has to buy a few newspapers and networks!"

"Which brings us to who set the bomb, Bobby," Quist said.

"I know. I'm supposed to be able to provide a possible answer," Bobby said, rubbing his bloodshot eyes with the palms of his hands. "I've been right beside Larry for almost

59

twenty-five years. I should be able to make an educated guess, shouldn't I?"

"And—?"

"I can't. I should be able to, but I can't. In all the time we've been together, I should know who was that kind of an enemy. It has to be somebody crazy, like a waiter or a taxi driver he didn't tip enough. Somebody with no more reason for it than that."

"That's a fun idea," Quist said after a moment, "but I don't buy it, Bobby. You know of any waiters or taxi drivers that were imported here to be part of Rainbow Hill's staff?"

"Mostly local," Bobby said. "Part of the business of creating good will in the community. There's Mr. Ricardo, of course. Larry hired him away from the Club Madrid in New York. Larry had known him there at the Madrid for many years and admired the way he dealt with the public. He couldn't have gotten a better man for the job. Now maybe that job doesn't exist."

"You think Larry won't go on with Rainbow Hill?"

Bobby's face seemed to crumple. "If he's alive he may."

"The reason I don't buy your psycho waiter or taxi driver is that this was so carefully planned in advance," Quist said. "The bomber had to know the whole layout, exactly where Larry would be located at the right time. Last night was chosen because it was a high point in Larry's career, the bringing to life of a dream. It was a perfect time to punish him, and only someone close to him would know that. The party last night, this place, mattered to Larry."

"The strange part of it is," Bobby said, "if he'd been in the cottage he'd never have known what hit him! There weren't even seconds for him to think, 'So-and-so is getting even with me!' Somebody just wanted him dead."

"And was here in advance to scout out the lay of the land, prepared with a bomb. You just don't buy a bomb at the corner drugstore on the spur of the moment. I keep getting the picture of someone who has held a grudge for a long time, nursed it and nourished it, and finally decided this was the right time to pay off."

"And muffed it on the first try," Bobby said. "He's not likely to blow it this second time, is he?"

"It's just possible we're wrong about that," Quist said. "I've been wondering if Larry could have taken off on his own, is hiding out because he can't make a case against someone he suspects. Until he can, he isn't going to make a target of himself a second time."

"You really think that could be? Oh, brother!" Bobby seemed to come alive again. "He would know, better than anyone, who might have an old grudge against him. Start spilling it, and the killer could be long gone before he could prove anything. So he stays in hiding—"

"The only problem is, Larry is one of the few people in the world who can't hide except in a hole in the ground. The whole world knows him, disguised or not, and they're all looking for him. He hasn't got a chance of operating out in the open to get the evidence he needs."

"So he just stays hidden," Bobby said. "He's got a million friends who would hide him if he asked. Wouldn't you, Mr. Quist?"

"I suppose I would," Quist said. His pale blue eyes were fixed steadily on Bobby. "So we have five people here who have known him a long time, would probably help him, hide him if he asked, and might just be able to dredge up the memory of some long-held grudge."

"Five people?"

"You, Bobby, the three ex-wives, and Mr. Ricardo. Are you hiding him, friend?"

"Oh, for God's sake, Mr. Quist!"

"One of you could be, and wouldn't talk if you were tortured. True friendship, true love."

A nerve twitched high up on Bobby's cheek. "If Larry

asked me to keep a secret I would," he said. "But he hasn't."

"So there are four others to ask," Quist said. "How much would you bet that they won't give me the same answer you have?"

Out in the lobby Dick Reeves, the network man, had set up a television camera and was interviewing the girl with the million-dollar legs, Beverly Jadwin, wife number two. A young fellow whom Quist recognized as one of Reeves's assistants stood near the camera.

"Dick's preparing a tape for the evening news," he said to Quist. "The three surviving ex-wives will make a lovely story. He's already done Sandra Ames."

The interview with Bev Jadwin was just about to begin.

"Don't hold the microphone up to your mouth, Miss Jadwin," Reeves was instructing the lady. "Keep it down lower or off to one side. It's strong enough to pick up whatever you have to say. Ready? When the red light shows on the camera, we're on the air." He raised his arm, brought it down, and the red light popped on. "It's very decent of you to join us at this tragic time, Miss Jadwin."

The woman's lips moved, but Quist couldn't hear anything. A polite whisper of some sort. He tried to remember what he knew about her. As a performer, a singer and dancer, she was still tops in her early forties, still striking looking. She had demonstrated her skills only last night with Larry. What she was like as a person, Quist didn't know. She'd been married once before Larry to a young bandleader who had disappeared over the years, and once after Larry to a Hollywood director who had faded into obscurity. Her one star performance in wedlock had been Larry.

"May I ask you first, Miss Jadwin, if you have any idea where Larry Lewis is now?" Reeves began his interview.

62

"If I did, I would have told the police," Bev said.

"You would also have told them if you had any notion of who had such a violent hatred for Larry."

"Of course—and I don't."

"You knew Glenda Forrest?"

"Of course." Bev was not looking directly at the camera. It would have revealed how deep her distress was.

"You know that she asked Larry for someplace where she could be private with a man friend. Do you have any idea who that man friend was? The police haven't been able to identify him yet."

"I don't know who he was. Glenda didn't share her private life with me, any more than I've shared mine with her."

"You must know how curious the public is about the party here last night, Miss Jadwin. A party at which a man's four ex-wives were all honored guests. You must none of you have any resentment toward the others or you wouldn't have been willing guests."

Bev shrugged. "It could have been just a way to have the spotlight turned on us, an important part of show business. Except for poor Glenda, who didn't want or need publicity."

"But that isn't why you came, is it?"

Bev raised her head and looked straight at the interviewer and the camera. "I came because Larry, in spite of our marital difficulties, has been a good and cherished friend over the years. He wanted me to come, and so I came."

"And you have no idea who could have hated him so much?"

"No idea." She sat very straight, obviously tense. "I would just like to say one thing. I would give anything to be able to answer that question, and I pray that the police will find Larry and catch the killer before it's too late."

63

Reeves was smart enough to recognize that he couldn't go much further with her. "I know how difficult this is for you, Miss Jadwin, and I'm grateful to you for talking with me. I think you know that we all pray for the same thing you do, Larry Lewis's safe return." He signaled to the cameraman and the red light went off. "Miss Payne is next. Please find her."

Bev Jadwin got up from the interview chair and started to move quickly away. Quist followed her till they were at the far end of the lobby. She turned, abruptly, to face him.

"Please, Quist, I've had all I can take," she said.

"Maybe you can help me find an answer to your prayer," Quist said. "I'm working on a theory that someone close to Larry is helping him hide."

She didn't respond but he saw that he had her hooked.

"There are some people very close to him here who would certainly help if he asked for it," Quist said. "There are you, and Sandra, and Patti Payne, and Bobby Crown, and possibly Ricardo. And there were many other people here last night who were good enough friends to respond to a cry for help if they heard it."

"Hiding him to keep him safe from the killer until the police catch him?" Bev asked.

"It could be."

Her dark eyes narrowed. "I hope to God you're right, Quist. If it's so, I'm not the one Larry asked. And I don't think he would have asked Sandra or Patti."

"Why?"

"You have to know Larry," she said. "I don't think he'd ask a woman for help, and certainly not one of us if it was dangerous."

"What about Bobby Crown or Ricardo?"

"They're both close enough," Bev said, "but neither one of them has left the Inn today. They'd have to hide him somewhere, and the troopers have been over the place from top to bottom. They could have supplied him with food, know where he is, I suppose."

"Someone else," Quist suggested. "A man who was at the party last night, someone I would have no reason to think of?"

"There was Mark Lawson, Larry's lawyer," Bev said. "But he was one of the first ones to get cleared and leave this morning. Larry was around after that, I'm almost certain. Mark had to get to town in a hurry because there was so much to handle for Larry—insurance and I suppose other finances."

"You can't think of anyone else?"

"You want to know what I really think?" Bev asked. "I think Larry could ask almost anyone for help, even a stranger, and get it. People love him, you know?"

"Well, thanks anyway," Quist said.

"I can't tell you how much I hope you're right," Bev said. "But I'm afraid, awfully afraid, that you're not. Right here, with all the police around him, would have been the safest place for Larry, wouldn't it?"

From across the lobby, Quist heard his name called loud and clear. He turned and saw his partner and closest friend, Dan Garvey, hurrying toward him.

2

Garvey, dark, intense, with a kind of electric energy, reached his friend, and for a moment his fingers, steely strong, gripped Quist's upper arms.

"I really steered you into a nightmare, didn't I, chum? Wading through reporters, I've picked up half a dozen conflicting stories. I got here as fast as I could—two speeding tickets along the way. What *is* the real story?"

"My room's on the second floor," Quist said. "Let's go there where we won't be interrupted."

Dan Garvey had been a star in his own right some years back. An all-American halfback at a Midwestern college, he'd gone on to be a headline-maker in professional football. Quist, early in his career as a public relations expert, had been hired to handle publicity for the owner of the team on which Garvey was the star performer. The two men got to be friends, and after a while Quist, sensing that his firm needed an expert in sports, someone who knew the sports writers and the ins and outs of professional athletics, offered Garvey a job when his football career had run its course. That was when the firm finally changed its name to Julian Quist Associates. It was more than a business partnership. The two men were the closest of friends.

"Tell me what really cooks, Julian," Garvey said when they reached Quist's room.

"Everyone has his own guess," Quist said. "The only fact that no one differs on is that Glenda Forrest was in Larry's cottage when someone blew it sky-high."

"With someone?"

"Not certainly identified." Quist told Garvey what Fred Forrest's theory was, a rescue mission by his man McNally that failed, as well as the second theory, that McNally had been Glenda's lover for the night.

"But that man's body hasn't been identified?"

"No, but McNally hasn't been found."

"And you buy the lover theory?"

"I tend to," Quist said. He went on to tell Garvey where Larry had been, with Madge Seaton. "The public story is that he was sleeping in a guest room."

"Not if it was the Larry I know," Garvey said. "I know that little jerk inside out." He smiled. "I use the word 'jerk' affectionately. He needs a woman every night just the way a kid needs his Wheaties for breakfast. It's not as ugly as it might sound. He makes no commitments, asks for none.

66

From what he tells me, in the spells where he was married he played it pretty straight; in between wives—and now— it's anyone looking for fun, no more, no less."

"Whoever blew up that cottage really wanted him dead," Quist said. "You knew him before you took on this job for him, didn't you?"

"Way back," Garvey said. "He was a sports nut, baseball in the summer, football in the fall and early winter. He used to say he took January off to get his wind back, and then in February the spring training begins for the big league baseball teams. He used to try to get nightclub jobs in Florida during February and March, just so he could watch the spring training games."

"Was he a gambler, Dan?" Quist asked.

Garvey laughed. "Compulsive, but not the way you mean, I think. 'Five bucks says the next girl who walks through that door will be a platinum blonde.' He would bet on anything—the weather, who played center field for the Detroit Tigers in 1909. You think up something to bet on, and he'd take it. But nothing big. Five bucks was about his limit, whether you were rich or poor."

"I've been wondering," Quist said. "I've talked to two of his wives, Sandra Ames and Bev Jadwin, to Bobby Crown, and to Ricardo, the maître d' he hired away from the Club Madrid. They all come up with an A-plus for Larry. 'Mr. Wonderful,' Martin, the county attorney, dubbed him."

"I guess I'd go along with that," Garvey said. "He's helped more people, contributed to more worthy causes than most of us and kept quiet about it. Never blows his own horn."

"This kind of violence doesn't seem to fit his world, his people. I've begun to wonder about gambling, drugs. It's kind of an underworld payoff, wouldn't you say?"

"Or someone who wanted it to look like that," Garvey said. "I tell you, there wasn't a day went by that he didn't make a nickel-and-dime bet. But nothing big."

"Maybe he kept that quiet, like his charities."

"I don't think so. And as for drugs, forget it. To stay where he is in his sixties, he's been a nut about physical fitness. He doesn't smoke, doesn't drink except for a glass of wine on some party occasion. He wouldn't have gone within a mile of drugs." Garvey hesitated. "Unless some friend of his was hooked, and he was trying to help."

"Let's try that on for size," Quist said. "A friend is on drugs, Larry finds out who the peddler is and turns him in."

"There'd be a police record of that somewhere."

"Bobby Crown might know," Quist said.

"Larry wouldn't gossip about a friend who was in trouble—unless he needed someone's help. He never talks about the women he's been involved with, and he wouldn't talk about a friend who was in trouble. That's the way he is."

Quist moved restlessly across the room. "Mr. Wonderful" seemed to get in the way of every notion he developed. "It doesn't smell like gangster to you, Dan?"

"It could be. But how do we get on the track of it until we can find Larry and get him to talk?"

"It isn't difficult to find out where he's been every minute of the last few years," Quist said. "Hollywood, Broadway, cities where he took a show on the road, nightclub engagements."

Garvey was frowning. "Crown could give us an itinerary for him. I know he did a stand in Reno."

"Gambling!" Quist said. "If we check back on him, we can hit police departments, the FBI. You willing to do that, Dan? I want to stay here."

"Why?"

"Because I could be wrong. But I'm beginning to smell a gangster payoff with every breath I take. It's their kind of violence."

"Okay, it's a deal," Garvey said. "I'll talk to Bobby Crown and take off with what he can give me."

Dick Reeves had just finished his interview with Patti Payne when Quist got back to the lobby. Larry Lewis hadn't run to a special type of woman, Quist thought. Sandra Ames was classic beauty and elegance, Bev Jadwin a sparkling showgirl type, the unfortunate Glenda a rich society girl with all the trappings of wealth. Patti Payne was a street kid grown up, brash, overly made-up, her blonde hair obviously dyed. He didn't have to track her down. She came straight toward him when she saw him across the lobby.

"Don't I get the treatment the other wives get?" she asked.

"Treatment?"

"You'll be giving out stories on all of us, won't you, Quist? I'd like what you say about me to be my own story," Patti said.

"I'm all ears," Quist said.

"We talk in public, everybody else in town will be all ears. You got a room or will you come to mine?"

"Lead the way," Quist said.

Patti's room was also on the second floor, just a couple of doors down the hall from Quist's. The dressing table, with a light mirror like a backstage dressing room's, was loaded with bottles, little jars, and tubes of cream. The scent of an exotic perfume was almost overpowering. Patti saw that his attention was fixed on it.

"That's the real me, there on the table, in case you didn't already know that," she said. "I do a pretty good job, considering what I have to start with. I was the homeliest girl on the street when I was growing up. That smart-assed broad you saw in the sketch with Larry last night is the real me, not Gracie Allen or anyone else."

"Damned amusing," Quist said.

"That's what Larry liked about me—likes about me," she said. "I wasn't pretending to be a romantic lovely like Sandra, or a copy of Ginger Rogers like Bev. I was just me, the kind of girl he grew up with. It took him a long time to select one of his own kind. After me, not Glenda or anyone else could make him feel at home."

"You just said that was you on the table," Quist said, gesturing toward the bottles and jars.

"Under lights, I'm a hag without that stuff," she said.

"I'm fascinated," Quist said, "but right now I'm not concerned with your makeup talents. What can you tell me that will help us find Larry? I have a feeling there's some kind of underworld connection with the bombing that no one's hit on yet."

"Underworld? Larry?" Her laugh was harsh. "If you go to church, Quist, Larry is an evil man. Women, women, women. But the rest of his life is downright moral. His friends are really friends. He's never had a knife out for anybody. He helps down-and-out people in his profession with benefit performances, he donates money to worthwhile causes. He's Mr. Nice Guy."

"Mr. Wonderful, the county attorney calls him. What about gambling, drugs?"

"You have to be kidding," she said. "He might bet you a buck on what color my hair would be the next time you saw me. That's the kind of gambling he did. When we were first married, I was taking some kind of pep pills. He blew his stack, washed them all down the toilet. He had no use for people who were on pills. You know something, Quist? I don't believe that bomb was meant for Larry."

"Glenda?"

"Who else? She got it, didn't she?"

"Nobody knew Glenda was in the cottage but Larry."

"Oh, come on, Quist, grow up," Patti said. "You think Larry would have left here last night, with all his famous guests and friends under his roof here, without someone knowing where to reach him? No matter who his lady was, someone would know how to reach him in case something went wrong."

"Went wrong?"

"Oh, a power failure, a fire, someone important had a medical emergency."

"I happen to know where he was," Quist said, "but he didn't tell anyone else beforehand. If he had, they'd have come forward."

"You just don't know Larry," Patti said. "He would help Glenda to shack up with some guy, he would go about his own romancing. But he wouldn't duck his responsibilities. I'll bet an arm he told Bobby Crown where he could be reached. Bobby is like that with Larry." She held up two crossed fingers.

"When the bomb went off, Bobby didn't tell anyone—if he knew."

"Why would he? Telling would hurt Larry's woman, whoever she is. Bobby knew Larry would turn up, sooner or later. He knew Larry wasn't in the cottage."

"And that Glenda was?"

"Probably. I'd say certainly. He didn't tell anyone in that first awful time because he knew Larry would turn up and give out the story he wanted to have told."

It made some sense, Quist thought. It was certainly worth exploring. "You knew Glenda well?" he asked Patti.

She gave an angry little shrug of her shoulders. "Too damn well," she said, closing her mouth in a tight, thin line. "She was the worst possible choice Larry could have made for himself. She played him for a sucker. She'd been having a kind of civil war with her father, for Lord knows how long. She used Larry as a weapon to get even with the old man. Forrest had busted up some relationship she cared about—for the moment, mind you—and Larry was too big in his own right for him to knock over with the back

71

of his hand. Larry served her purpose, and after a few months she walked out on him. It hurt Larry to have been used like that."

"And yet he invited her here to his party and set up a love nest for her?"

"That's Larry," Patti said. "Bev has called him an 'old mother hen.' Larry has taken care of Sandra and Bev and me, and even Glenda, as though we were his kids, not his ex-lovers and wives. 'Buy me a lollipop, Daddy,' and Larry would do anything for any of us who asked for something." She tried on her bitter smile. "I needed help with something once—something he had no reason to help me with— and he told me, 'You've got my mark on you, kiddo,' he said. 'I don't want anyone to find you in a jam with my mark on you. I take care of my own, past and present.'"

"A pretty complex character," Quist said. "So let's try to put some of the pieces of your puzzle together. Bobby Crown knew that Glenda was in the cottage and where Larry was. He probably knew those things fairly early in the evening. He lets what he knows slip to somebody."

"Never," Patti said. "Not Bobby. Anything Larry told Bobby in confidence was as safe as if it were locked in a bank vault. But anyone who had an eye on Glenda could have seen her go to the cottage. That must have been while the party was going full blast, because she never showed up at the party. There would have been all kinds of time for him to plant a bomb."

"That couldn't have been Paul Powers, who is Forrest's man, could it? He didn't show up at the party either."

"You'd have to invent some kind of motive for him," Patti said. "He stood to lose too much by knocking her off. He was her old man's choice for her, and a few million bucks when he chose to get generous."

"Then who, Patti?"

"Glenda wasn't my kind of woman," Patti said. "She played the field, both before, during and after she was

72

married to Larry. There must have been ten guys at the party who'd been in the hay with her at one time or another. She was everyone's girl. I guess there were guys who wanted her just because she *did* have Larry's 'mark' on her."

"Has that been true with you?"

"You mean men who were after me because I'd once been Larry's woman? I suppose so. I don't think I ever fell for it."

"But you can't suggest anyone who would kill her because she was sleeping with somebody else?"

"Do you know anyone who is that crazy, Quist? There is someone, of course, but *who* is beyond me."

"Larry?" Quist suggested. "If he was being a mother hen to Glenda, he might make a guess. That would explain what's happened to him, wouldn't it? He goes to the man he suspects and gets himself behind the eight ball."

Patti seemed to grow tense again for a moment, her fingers intertwined and locked together, her knuckles white. Then she relaxed and began flexing those fingers. "I don't think so," she said.

"It would be logical."

"You don't know Larry the way I do, Quist. You can't grow up just a little over five feet tall, with all the men in the world towering over you, and go looking for trouble. That explains a lot of things about Larry. He wasn't any good in a barroom brawl, but he could outperform those big men, outsucceed them, outdo them with women. He couldn't trade a punch in the eye with some big guy, but he could outrun him at any other game. That's Larry."

"It's impertinent of me to ask," Quist said, "but I've thought that because Larry was like a little kid in size, that women's maternal instincts started to work overtime. Was it that way, Patti?"

Patti laughed. "Let me tell you something, Quist. That little man has so much sexual electricity, sexual energy, that it rolls over you like a runaway truck! I promise you I never felt maternal about him, and I doubt if I ever will, or could!"

Quist drew a deep breath. "So he wouldn't go to someone he suspected of murder. Not his technique for dealing with physical danger. But the crazy man you suggest, the one who would blow up Glenda and her lover, might go after Larry for helping Glenda to have what she wanted."

"But who, damn it? Who?" Patti said. "We've got to find him, Quist. There still may be time—"

Quist nodded, though he didn't have much hope that time was on their side. "I tell you what, luv. You talk to Sandra and Bev. They may have some clue to Glenda's recent romances that has escaped you. I'll tackle Bobby Crown, and then we can check back."

When they reached the lobby again, some instinct told Quist that there was a new excitement of some kind— something else. Bobby Crown was no longer at the front desk, and troopers moved quickly from the rear office that Captain Shannon and Andrew Martin had taken over and headed out the various front entrances. He headed for the office. The door was open, but a trooper barred his way. Beyond, he could see Shannon and Martin engaged in a conversation with Bobby Crown. Martin saw him and called out to the trooper.

"You can let Mr. Quist in, Toby." Then, as Quist approached: "You might as well know what's cooking from the horse's mouth. We've discovered where the explosives came from that blew up the cottage."

"Any news of Larry?" Quist asked. That came first with him.

"Nothing, unfortunately," Martin said. "We've been calling it a bomb. Now we believe it was a couple of dozen sticks of dynamite planted all around the foundation, set off by a discharger from some distance away."

74

"Which helps us how?" Quist asked.

"We've been thinking of someone bringing in a bomb from somewhere away from here." Shannon said. "Now we know a large supply of dynamite was stolen from right here on the property."

"Why was dynamite stored here?" Quist asked.

Bobby Crown answered the question, his haggard face twitching with fatigue. It seemed that Larry had planned to enlarge the swimming pool at the south end of the Inn. They hadn't gotten to it before the date for the party arrived. It couldn't be finished ahead of time in any event. The explosives to be used for blasting were stored in a toolshed at the site, locked in a large metal-bound box. A little while ago, one of the contractor's men, curious about the explosion, checked the toolshed and found the box broken open, the lock smashed, and a couple of dozen sticks of dynamite, plus blasting caps and a detonator, all missing.

"Two and two," Andrew Martin said. "Explosives experts are double-checking now, knowing what they're looking for. But there doesn't seem to be much doubt that that's the source of the explosives."

"Which changes what?" Quist asked.

"It gives it a kind of a local twist," Martin said. "Most of the guests at the party came from out of town, had never been here before. They wouldn't know about Larry's plans for the future, wouldn't know about stored dynamite or where it was kept. Local workmen would have known, people on the Inn's staff could have known."

"It would be someone who knew where it was, how to plant it, how to hook up the detonator and shoot it off," Shannon said.

"It doesn't sound like one of the show-business crowd who were the guests."

"You knew the stuff was there, Bobby?" Quist asked.

Crown nodded. "Knew it was there, discussed it with

75

Larry. Was it safe to leave it there, with the Inn crowded? Larry just laughed and asked if I knew anybody on the guest list who might want to blow up the joint. The stuff was locked away, good strong padlock. You wouldn't come on it by accident, and there was nothing on the box that indicated what was stored in it."

"The person who went after the stuff had to know it was there," Shannon said.

"What concerns me, and I'm sure you, Bobby, is where is Larry? I've just been talking to Patti Payne, and she has an interesting notion."

"That's Mrs. Larry Number Three?" Andrew Martin asked.

Quist nodded. "We've all been assuming the bomber was after Larry and didn't know that Glenda was in the cottage. Patti thinks Glenda may have been the target all along."

"I toyed with that early on," Martin said. "But there wasn't anything to support it. Larry Lewis was sure he was the target when he talked to Captain Shannon."

"But couldn't come up with a guess as to who had it in for him," Quist said. "Larry is still Mr. Wonderful to anyone who talks about him. Patti, at least, doesn't have anything good to say about Glenda. What about her, Bobby? You had to know her as well as anybody except Larry himself."

Bobby lifted the palms of his hands to his eyes again. He couldn't go on much further without some rest, Quist thought. "I started to handle Larry's business affairs just when he was breaking up with Bev Jadwin. I got to know Bev and Sandra later, but not as closely as I knew Patti when she became number three. I know her best of all. Glenda was only Mrs. L. for a few months."

"But in that time did you know anyone who might have hated her enough to plan to wipe her out?" Quist asked.

"It's a funny thing," Bobby said, shaking his head as though it were hard for him to concentrate on the question. "You grow up and live in one kind of world. You understand the people in your world because they think the way you do, or do what they do for reasons that you understand. I'm ten years younger than Larry. Even when I was growing up, because I was a little guy like Larry, I dreamed I could make it like he had." His voice was bitter. "I guess I've never had what he had, but I was determined to try. I got a job as a stand-in for him in one of his films. I was the right size. I thought I might learn from him. What I learned from him was that I could never match his talents."

"You're drifting away from Glenda," Martin said.

"I know," Bobby said. "I'm trying to explain why I'm not much help when it comes to her. You see, she didn't belong in my world, the world of show business. She didn't understand us any better than I understood her."

"Patti suggests that she was a pretty promiscuous lady," Quist said.

"Like a rabbit!" Bobby said, his voice suddenly sharp. "Larry never ran into anything like that with his other ladies. It burned him. It got people talking about him, that he'd lost his special ability to hang on to a woman for as long as he wanted. Not only that, Glenda wasn't interested in show business. She wanted him to quit, invest in a ranch somewhere, stop being a star where he was."

"Could he have resented that enough to decide to polish her off when she asked him to arrange a love session with someone else for her?" Shannon asked.

"Never!" Bobby said. "It didn't work, they separated, he couldn't have cared less what she did with her life."

"Even helped her to do it?"

"Even that," Bobby said. "He might have laughed about it later on, but kill her for it, never!" His smile returned. "He might have thought it was fun to help her have an affair with her father's chauffeur and spy. Serve the old bastard right!"

"If it wasn't McNally, you have no idea who it might have been?" Martin asked.

"She'd moved in and out of my world in a hurry," Bobby said. "I had no reason to keep tabs on her once she was out of Larry's life."

"Someone who was here for the party," Shannon said. "Someone who saw her go to the cottage with McNally. Someone who blew them both to hell and gone and then went after Larry Lewis to punish him for having helped her do what she was doing."

"I can't even make a guess," Bobby said.

"So we have two games to play, but which is the right one?" Shannon asked, his voice angry.

"Trying to guess doesn't help us find Larry," Quist said. "If the explosives from that toolshed were used to blow up the cottage, that, as you have said, suggests it was someone local, attached to the Inn in some way. That suggests that Larry hasn't been taken out of the area. The killer couldn't leave here without being missed."

"We just keep covering the countryside, the woods," Shannon said. "A body can be hidden under dead leaves, or brush, and be missed the first time around. We just have to keep going over and over the ground until we find him. We've got dogs working now."

"I just can't believe he's dead," Bobby Crown said, his voice unsteady. "He could be hiding somewhere, couldn't he?"

"Why would he hide?" Martin asked. "All he has to do is come to us, tell us what's cooking, and he's safe. I'm afraid I don't think we're going to see him alive again."

"I just won't buy that!" Bobby said.

"You mean you can't bear to buy it," Martin said. He turned to Quist. "I think we're done with your theory about gambling, drugs, and the underworld, Quist. The underworld would have come bringing their own weapons, with a definite plan. They wouldn't have improvised once they got here."

Bobby Crown lifted his heavy eyelids to look at Quist.

"Dan Garvey asked me about gambling and drugs. I told him no way. I don't think he believed me, but I still say— no way."

Two games to play, Shannon had said. Either Larry Lewis had been the target for the killer and Glenda was killed by mistake or Glenda had been the target and no mistake at all had been made. The gangster theory didn't make much sense with the discovery of the source of the explosives.

Quist went looking for Patti, just about convinced that her theory was the correct one. Glenda had been the target, and Larry was missing, not because he knew something but because, in someone's sick mind, he had conspired with Glenda to get her involved with the wrong man.

Quist didn't see Patti anywhere, but Sandra Ames was sitting alone in one of the lobby armchairs. She seemed glad to see Quist, as though being alone was a new experience for her. He sat down in the chair next to hers and brought her up to date on the discovery of the source of the explosives and what the implications were—someone local who knew where to find the means of destruction.

"Patti has been talking to Bev and me," Sandra said. "This makes her guess pretty solid, doesn't it?"

"It certainly needs running down," Quist said. "Did you girls come up with anything interesting about Glenda?"

Sandra shook her head slowly. "There are two things you need to understand, Quist. Bev and I are too far back down the tracks—Larry's tracks—to pay very much attention to the private life of a girl two stops further on. Curiosity, you think? My run on this road, Julian, has been a forty-year stretch. Early on I was curious about Bev when she got Larry. Later I was just a little curious about Patti, mainly because I hadn't thought she was Larry's type. But Glenda, not really. People still gossip to me about Larry, as if we hadn't been separated for thirty-five years. Of course we haven't, in a way. We've been friends all that time. What I heard about Glenda turned me off. She was a freewheeling slut, from everything I was told. I thought it would be a short run for Larry, and it was. After that I couldn't have cared less about what went on in Glenda's life. I didn't care, I didn't listen, I didn't hear. So I can't help now."

"Is it the same with Bev?"

"Pretty much, I think. None of us, Patti included, could remember hearing about anyone special in Glenda's current life. None of us cared. We might have if we thought her style bothered Larry, but it didn't."

"So we draw a blank," Quist said.

"Patti had a bright idea," Sandra said. "She's gone to check with Mr. Ricardo, the old maître d' at the Club Madrid. The Madrid was a special hangout of Glenda's. That's where Larry met her, you know. Ricardo could know about men in Glenda's life we never even heard of." Sandra's eyes narrowed as if she felt a sudden pain. "No news of Larry?"

"Neither good nor bad," Quist said.

The young man who was filling in for Bobby Crown at the front desk told Quist he could probably find Mr. Ricardo in the dining room. "Most of the guests have left," the young man said, "but an army of reporters and television people have taken over. We seem to be serving meals around the clock."

The dining room was busy, with Mr. Ricardo, like a majestic traffic cop, in charge. He stood by a sort of standing desk at the entrance to the room, a professional smile on his dark, handsome face.

Patti had caught up with him, but they hadn't talked at any length. Things had been spinning here in the dining room, and Patti had said she needed to freshen up and would be back in half an hour.

"As if time weren't important," Quist said, sounding grim.

80

"She said she wanted to ask about the unfortunate Glenda Forrest," Ricardo said. "Could I report on any special lover from the past who might have been among last night's party guests."

"And could you?"

"My job is peculiar," Ricardo said. "Has been for many years. I have been, you might say, the host at a party every night of my life, hundreds of people passing by me, saying hello. Checking on reservations. 'I'm at Mr. So-and-so's table.' You know him, when he comes the next time, as a friend of Mr. So-and-so's, but you don't necessarily know his name. Guests of the management, famous people, you know, but hundreds of them are just familiar faces."

"But you knew Glenda Forrest."

"Oh, certainly. Reservations for her at the Madrid were always in her name. Most of the young men who came in with her were just 'one of Glenda's guys.' Show me a face, and I'll remember where I saw it before. Names, I'd need a giant computer to keep a record of them."

"No one stands out, then, among Glenda's boyfriends, who was also here last night? You'd remember the face, even if you couldn't name him."

Ricardo shook his head slowly. "There was no one here last night that I associate with Glenda in the Madrid days. Oh, this morning I saw that Paul Powers, but I didn't see him at the party last night. He came to the Madrid a couple of times in the old days. I promised Miss Payne I'd keep thinking, someone who seemed to be special to Glenda in the past. I'm not hopeful that I can tie any such memory into Rainbow Hill last night."

"Gossip?" Quist suggested.

Mr. Ricardo smiled his very white smile. "In my business, Mr. Quist, it's like being in a blizzard. Snowflakes everywhere, and you don't stop to try to identify one from the other. In one ear and out the other, unless it was about your own sister or mother. As for Glenda Forrest, I'm reminded of a football team running out of the locker room before the start of the game, following their captain or coach. Glenda was the captain, and the rest were just a lot of young men with numbers on their backs."

"You remembered the night Larry met her, broke up some kind of brawl between Glenda's young man and her father. The police came—"

"I remember it because it was Larry. He could distract a burglar from a lock he was trying to pick."

"But the young man the row was about?"

"You can forget him," Ricardo said. "His name was Jerome Crawford. Old man Forrest hid him away somewhere overseas in some faraway corporate job. I never saw him again. He certainly wasn't here last night."

"Well, that seems to be that," Quist said. "Keep trying, Ricardo. Something may click into place for you if you keep at it. I'll get back to you."

"Don't count on me, Mr. Quist. Now that the police have found out where the explosives came from, they think it was someone local. But that's a puzzle, too."

"In what way?"

"I know that Glenda arrived here at Rainbow Hill yesterday afternoon about three o'clock. She'd never been here before. She wanted a tour of the place, and I heard Larry promise he'd find someone to take her around the whole establishment, the golf course, the works. She hadn't had time to make a contact with anyone local. Not someone who would get so involved he would blow her to pieces in the next fifteen hours or so. That's why I think the bombing, so-called, was meant for Larry, and having missed him with that, the killer has made a second try. Glenda Forrest was playing with fire, but I don't think it was this kind of fire."

Round and round the mulberry bush, Quist thought. He decided he would try to contact Patti and catch her up on the dynamite discovery and Mr. Ricardo's thoughts on the

82

subject. He tried calling her room on the house phone but she didn't answer. He realized that he hadn't stopped to shave since the explosion had waked him early that morning and that he'd grown a pretty healthy stubble on his chin. He decided to go up to his own room and freshen up.

On the second floor he walked down the hall and almost past the door of Patti's room, when he saw that her door was standing an inch or two ajar. She could, he thought, have been in the shower and not heard the phone.

He knocked, and when there was no answer he pushed the door a little wider open and called out, "Patti? It's Julian Quist."

When there was still no answer, he pushed the door open still wider and took a step into the room. He heard his breath whistling through his teeth as he stared at what he saw there. He reached out to steady himself on the side of the door.

Lying spread-eagled on the floor in the center of the room was Patti. The dyed blonde hair was unmistakable, although her face seemed to have been mangled, slashed. Her mouth was bloody and gaping open. The front of her blouse was smeared with red.

He took a step closer, speaking her name again, but in a whisper: "Patti!"

And then he saw that her throat had been cut from ear to ear. He knelt beside her, but he didn't touch her. He knew at once that this was a police matter, not a medical problem. Lying on the floor beside her was a small piece of something that looked like bloody meat.

Then he stood up and turned away, fighting a wave of terrible nausea. The bloody piece of meat on the floor beside the body was Patti's tongue.

PART THREE

PART
THREE

1

Even long afterward, Quist didr't have a clear memory of what he did in the next few minutes. He must have acted in a kind of shocked trance. He apparently called down an alarm to Captain Shannon on Patti's phone and then stood guard over the remains of a woman who had been vibrantly alive only a little while ago, struggling to recover from what had been like a violent blow to his solar plexus. He was in the presence of a kind of awful violence that could only spring out of madness.

He did remember standing, frozen, looking around for the weapon that had been used to butcher the lady he'd been talking with so recently. There was no sign of it. Unless it was somehow hidden under the body, the murderer must have taken it with him

Suddenly the whole world seemed to pour into the room: Captain Shannon, three other troopers, Andrew Martin, and a dark-haired stranger whom Quist didn't know but who seemed to have some authority. Outside the hall, barred from the room by another trooper, reporters clamored to be admitted to the horror.

Quist answered a quick question from the dark-haired stranger. He had touched nothing but the telephone. No one had to be told that there was nothing that could be done for the woman.

"Son of a bitch cut out her tongue!" someone said in a shocked voice.

Quist, his mouth feeling as stiff as if it had been para-lyzed by Novocaine, explained that Mr. Ricardo had told him Patti had gone to her room to freshen up, that he'd noticed the door ajar, had knocked, called out to Patti, and when she didn't answer, had stepped into the room.

"You passed no one in the hall as you were approaching her door?" the dark stranger asked. It turned out later that his name was Frank Sloan, a homicide detective from trooper headquarters, who had only just arrived on the scene. Quist had seen no one.

"You must have missed him by only a minute or two. This slaughter is that fresh," Shannon said.

Quist walked over to the window. The thing he wanted most in the world was to get away from this. The window looked down over the back garden where the charred remains of the cottage were plainly visible in the approaching twilight. There was no escape from the evidence of mayhem.

Andrew Martin came up behind Quist and put a comforting hand on his shoulder. "I've got a bottle of Jack Daniel's in my room just down the hall," he said. "You look like a man who could use a shot in the arm."

Quist nodded, and Martin started to guide him toward the door.

"Don't get lost, Quist," Captain Shannon said. "We'll need to go over this with you when we've checked out here."

The reporters in the hall didn't want to let them pass, but Martin just told them "Later!" and ran a kind of interference for Quist. In Martin's room, which was a neat duplicate of Quist's, the lawyer went to the bureau and produced the bottle of whiskey he'd promised. He poured some in a tumbler from the bathroom and handed it to Quist.

"Can't do you anything but good," he said.

Quist sat down on the edge of the bed because his legs felt as though they might buckle under him. He sipped the whiskey and sensed that his heart was still beating.

"The smell of blood," he said. "So sickly sweet!"

"You want to practice on me?" Martin asked. "Shannon and Sloan, the homicide guy, are going to want every minor detail you've got."

Quist put down the glass on the bedside table, shaking his head to the gestured offer of another drink. "If Shannon is right about my just missing him, the monster who did that must be still close enough for us to reach out and grab him."

"No one is going to walk away," Martin said. "There's an army of troopers and the local sheriff and his deputies surrounding the Inn. Problem is, who are they looking for?"

"There's no way anyone can have done what was done in there and not be smeared with blood himself," Quist said.

Martin's face was twisted by a look of revulsion. "That tongue! A madman's message on what will happen to someone who has something to tell! You know what it can have been that she knew, Quist?"

"I know what she was looking for, but she hadn't found it less than an hour ago," Quist said. "She was looking for some former lover of Glenda Forrest's who might have blown up the cottage when she went there with another man. She hadn't come up with a name after talking to Sandra and Bev. She left them to go upstairs to freshen up. I talked to Sandra after she'd left. None of them had come up with a guess. I headed up to my room to shave, passed Patti's door and saw it was open, looked in when she didn't answer. She couldn't have been upstairs more than fifteen minutes!"

"In that time she came up with a name and the guy stopped her from passing it on," Martin said.

"But she didn't have a name. Not when she left Sandra and Bev."

"Right now I'm living in a world of 'could-have-beens,'" Martin said. "She didn't have a name when she went up to her room. Someone came there to see her, and when she saw him something clicked for her. 'You're it!' she tells him. He makes sure she doesn't tell anyone else."

"Being ready with a knife?"

Martin nodded. "This madman is ready for super-violence any time he wants to act."

"So now he's wandering around, spattered with Patti's blood."

"This character knows the Inn like a book," Martin said. "He knew where her room was, he knew where the dynamite was stored yesterday. He may have a room here himself and be able to make a quick change of clothes."

"And what does he do with the bloodstained ones?"

"Knowing the Inn as well as he does, he'd know where there's an incinerator where he could dispose of them," Martin said. His smile was twisted. "That's all a 'could-have-been,' you understand. There's not one shred of evidence to back it up. So let me throw you one more curve, chum. We now have two dead ex-wives. How safe are the other two?"

Quist guessed what was coming, opened his mouth to protest, and then changed his mind. "Let's put away your crystal ball," he said. "It comes up with too many conflicting pictures to be accurate."

"You don't want to play the Larry Lewis game?" Martin asked.

"Because it's too far out," Quist said.

"He invited his four ex-wives here. Two of them are gone. Did he invite them all here for a mass revenge of some sort?"

Quist almost laughed. "If I ever find myself promoting some television soap opera, I promise I'll recommend you as a writer, Martin. Larry can't wander around this hotel killing people. He can't go two feet without being recognized, and everyone's looking for him."

"The man is an actor," Martin said. "A bellhop's uniform? A maintenance man's work apron? A chauffeur's uniform?"

"So the other bellhops would know he was a fake. So would the maintenance men and the chauffeurs. And they're all looking for Larry Lewis. All their jobs depend on finding him alive and well. And what possible motive can you dream up for Larry?"

"No one can dream up a motive for this killer, whoever he is, except his psychiatrist, if he's got one," Martin said.

"I think I'll leave you to your dreams," Quist said. "Sandra and Bev are going to be hit where they live when they hear about Patti. They'll need some kind of support." He started for the door and stopped. "Let me add to your 'could-have-beens,' Martin. Someone is out to get Larry and the four people he really cared for. He now has only two to go. You care for that?"

Quist realized he should have known he wouldn't have to break the news to anyone. Word of this new horror had swept through the Inn like a brushfire. He almost had to fight his way through the reporters out in the hall. He couldn't tell them anything they did not already know. At the foot of the stairs he found himself faced by Mr. Ricardo. The "Spanish nobleman" had left his post. He looked shaken.

"Is it true that you found her, Mr. Quist?"

Quist nodded.

"Is it true what they say—stabbed, her throat cut, her tongue—?"

"A bloodbath," Quist said.

"Santa Maria!" Ricardo whispered "Is anyone connected with Larry Lewis safe?"

"If you know something you're not telling, you may not be," Quist said.

"Before God, I told the police all I know," Ricardo said. "But nobody has the handle on this, do they? They don't know where to start!"

"It starts with a hate so deep you can't give it a name. But who hates who for what?" Quist glanced across the lobby. Sandra and Bev were there, surrounded by a little group of people, a couple of whom Quist recognized as reporters. Two state troopers were standing near the two ex-wives. As he approached the group, they all faced him, looking eager for the real story.

"There's nothing I can tell you, or have the stomach to tell you, that you haven't already heard," Quist said. "If anything, it's uglier than anything you've been told."

Sandra, her face the color of ashes, reached out to him. "Can you tell us why these two troopers have been assigned to protect Bev and me, Julian?"

"Larry is gone, Glenda is gone, Patti is gone," he said. "It takes on a shape that Captain Shannon can't ignore."

Questions were fired at him from the little group; as if from a scatter-gun. Quist held up his hands to try to silence them. "I can't answer questions until I've made a statement to the police," he said. "I'd very much like to talk to Miss Ames and Miss Jadwin in private. There's a little card room across the way there." He glanced at the troopers. "Can we go there?"

"With us," one of the troopers said.

The card room was deserted. The two troopers stationed themselves at the door, one on the outside and one inside the room. Quist and the two ladies retreated to the circular poker table at the far end of the room.

"What kind of 'shape' were you talking about out there?" Bev Jadwin asked before they were seated.

Quist wondered how to tell them. "Right now there isn't

one scrap of solid evidence anywhere, so everyone is playing guessing games," Quist said. "Guess number one is that the bombing of the cottage was meant for Larry, with the killer having no way of knowing that Larry had loaned the cottage to Glenda. Guess number two is that Glenda was meant to die, along with her lover. Guess number three—it was meant for Larry, failed, and now the killer has taken a second go at Larry. Guess number four—it was meant for Glenda, Larry is being punished for setting up the arrangement for the lovers, and Patti has been silenced because she remembered who a jealous lover of Glenda's might be."

"None of those explains why Sandra and I are suddenly under police protection," Bev said.

Quist gave her a steady look. "So we come to guess number five," he said. "Fasten your seatbelts! Larry gathered his four ex-wives here under one roof, with some kind of psychotic reason for eliminating all four of you, one by one."

Bev Jadwin actually laughed. "Oh, brother!" she said. "Guess number six is that it's a man from Mars!"

Sandra moved her lips before she spoke, as if they were frozen. "Someone has actually put that craziness into words?"

"When you have nothing to go on, you reach out for anything," Quist said. "I took it a step further when I heard it. Not Larry gone crazy, but someone else who intends to wipe out Larry and all the women who have been part of his life. Larry is missing. Evidently I'd rather think he's dead than gone mad."

"It's all absurd," Bev said. "Glenda was the intended victim. Larry guessed who it is and has been silenced. Patti guessed who it is—"

"There you go, like everyone else, guessing," Quist said. "How come neither Larry nor Patti mentioned their suspicions to anyone else?"

"They confronted the killer with their suspicions," Bev said.

Quist shook his head. "Would you walk up to a person you know must be psychotic and tell him you suspect him of murder? Neither Larry nor Patti would be that dim-witted."

"They could both have gone to the same person, told him something they suspected, and that person knew that what they suspected would sooner or later lead to him."

"They wouldn't guess that what they suspected might lead to the person they were talking to?" Quist asked.

"They would both trust the same person," Bev said.

"Since it wasn't me," Sandra said, "and it wasn't Bev, I can only think of three people Larry and Patti might trust totally." She turned to Quist. "You, Julian, your partner Dan Garvey, and Bobby Crown."

Quist nodded, as though he took it quite seriously. "So since it wasn't you, and it wasn't Bev, and it wasn't Dan—who isn't here, by the way—and it isn't me, that leaves Bobby."

"The one person I know who would lie down on the railroad tracks and let a train run over him if he thought it would help Larry," Bev said.

Even as she was speaking, the door to the card room opened and the outside trooper ushered in Bobby Crown, looking near death from fatigue. Bev greeted him.

"We've just made guess number seven, or seven hundred, Bobby," Bev said. "You are the killer!"

Bobby didn't seem to hear. "The law wants to get a statement from you, Julian. I was sent to find you."

"Before you go, Julian," Sandra said.

"Yes?"

"Someone's got to represent Larry's interests here, and mine, and Bev's," she said. "You and Bobby are the only ones we can count on. Find Larry! Find out the true facts about Glenda. Let the law play these absurd guessing games. Represent us—please, Julian! I don't have to ask Bobby, but he can tell you everything there is to know about this place, about the past, about Larry's affairs! Please! You two can be miles ahead of the cops if you'll try."

"You don't really have to ask, luv," Quist said. "You're right, of course. These guessing games are for the birds."

As they walked across the lobby toward the office where the police were established, Bobby Crown moved with his head down, as if he didn't want to see or be seen by anyone.

"You heard what Bev said when you came into the card room?" Quist asked. "A guess that you are the killer?"

"Bev is a great one-line comic," Bobby said.

The atmosphere in the office was one of tension and frustration. Lights were on, as night had fallen, and little circles of tobacco smoke drifted over the lamps. Shannon, Andrew Martin, and Sloan, the homicide detective, were there. A trooper was stationed at a stenotype machine.

"We've written down your original statement, Mr. Quist," Shannon said. "Take a look at it, will you? If it's all right as it stands, we can save some time." He handed a sheet of paper to Quist.

The statement was brief and accurate. He had been going to his own room when he noticed that Patti's door was standing an inch or so open. He had knocked, gotten no answer, opened the door, and seen Patti lying there, murdered. He had sounded the alarm and waited for the cops.

"It's accurate," Quist said.

"If you'll sign it, please. And now, questions."

Quist signed the statement and waited.

"You weren't looking for Miss Payne when you went upstairs?" Shannon asked.

"Yes and no," Quist said. "I was actually going upstairs to

shave, but I'd been looking for Patti. We'd been discussing Glenda, and there was a chance she might have remembered something. Miss Ames had told me Patti'd gone up to her room and when I saw the door ajar—" Quist shrugged.

"What had you expected she could remember?"

"The name of some former lover of Glenda's who could have been jealous enough to blast the cottage."

"She hadn't come up with any suggestion?"

"No. Nothing even close."

"When you went upstairs and started down the hall, did you pass anyone, see anyone leaving that second floor?"

"I don't think so. I don't remember."

"You find a dead woman, butchered, and you don't remember?" Sloan, the homicide man, asked in a harsh voice.

"People have been circulating everywhere in this Inn," Quist said. "Somebody could have passed me, and I might not have noticed. I wasn't paying attention. Had no reason to. But I don't remember seeing anyone."

"In your conversations with Miss Payne, did she suggest she was afraid of anyone?"

"No."

"But you were working on the theory that the explosion in the cottage was meant for Glenda Forrest?"

"It was one of your suggestions. I thought it was worth checking out. Aside from Bobby, here, Patti was the person most likely to know something about Glenda that might help."

Shannon made a little helpless gesture and turned away, indicating to Martin and Sloan that Quist was their pigeon. Sloan, his face dark as a thundercloud, took over.

"You've been in the cottage, Quist?" he asked.

"Yesterday afternoon when I first arrived," Quist said. "Captain Shannon knows I was there, saw Larry and

Glenda Forrest, and witnessed an encounter with Paul Powers. That's the only time I was ever in the cottage."

"I know that's what you've said but that isn't why I asked you the question. We're convinced now that the stolen dynamite was used to blow up the cottage. It would take some time, don't you think, to plant a couple of dozen sticks of dynamite around the cottage foundation?"

"I suppose it would."

Sloan seemed to relax a little. "Captain Shannon leans toward the idea that the explosion was meant for Glenda Forrest. I think, because of the time it would have taken to plant those sticks of dynamite, that it was done well in advance, sometime during the day or night before, and therefore intended for Larry Lewis. There were two hundred people here for the party last night. No one would have risked trying to plant that dynamite with so many people around—people wandering out into the garden on a warm summer night."

"Are you asking me what I think?" Quist asked.

"Not really, unless you have facts you haven't given us." Sloan said.

"Can I ask a question?"

"Shoot."

"If the dynamite was stolen from the toolshed out by the pool a couple of days ago, wouldn't it have been missed?" Quist asked.

Sloan gestured to Bobby Crown.

Bobby drew a deep breath, as though it took an effort to speak. "Larry had hoped to have the swimming pool enlarged by the time of the party," he said. "But it became obvious the work couldn't be finished in time. Larry didn't want to start the blasting and just have a hole in the ground when his guests arrived. So it was decided to delay that work, and the dynamite was locked away."

"It wasn't checked on?"

"No reason to check on it—till after the explosion," Bobby said.

"But I understand the lock was broken on the box that contained the dynamite," Quist said. "Wouldn't that have been noticed?"

Sloan answered that one. "According to the contractor, with the work postponed on the pool there was no reason for anyone to have gone into the shed. Everything that was stored there related to the work on the pool. They only looked in there after the explosion. So I think it was set up well in advance, planned to be set off when all of Lewis's friends were here. Killer didn't know that he'd loaned the cottage to his ex-wife."

"But you're still guessing, aren't you, Sloan?"

"Yes, damn it, but it's a pretty solid guess, I think."

Andrew Martin smiled at Quist. Nothing seemed to disturb his good humor. "The problem is, all three of us are headed in different directions. I don't buy this Mr. Wonderful dream up. Lewis had four marriages. None of them worked, so he can't be so wonderful. He's got a million fans, all of whom are supposed to love him, but if he isn't so wonderful, any one of them could be harboring a deep resentment that we have no way of knowing about. And if he isn't so wonderful, he could be mad as a hatter. He buys an Inn, sets up the party of the century, persuades all his marriage failures to attend, and then puts on the performance of a lifetime. Two of the ladies are dead, and two remain. And as far as we know, he's somewhere ready to strike again, while we sit around chewing our fingernails. So my guess is that Larry Lewis is the villain of the piece. He had all kinds of time, nights before anybody came to his party, to set up the death trap in the cottage. If Glenda hadn't asked for the use of the cottage, he'd have found a way to offer it to her. In my book, until we find Lewis, the game isn't over."

"That's all absolutely insane," Bobby Crown muttered.

"Exactly my theory," Martin said. "We're dealing with a crazy man and we've got to guard against more craziness. You got a reaction, Quist?"

Quist hesitated, frowning. "Finding Larry should be at the top of everyone's list," he said. "If we find him dead, that will blow your theory, Martin, and the captain's theory that Glenda was the target. If we find him alive—" Quist shrugged. "In that case the explanations will have to come from him. If he were here, walking around among us, you'd never suspect him for a minute. Why would he hide out and draw attention to himself if he plans to go on killing? Even a psycho would have more sense than to draw attention to himself before he's finished what he planned."

"Just the way I think," Sloan said. "He's dead, and the ballgame is over as far as guessing is concerned. But we still don't have any lead to who was out to get him."

"At this point you wouldn't like me to throw one at you, would you?" Quist asked.

The three men looked at him, interested. Anything that they hadn't chewed over and over could be helpful.

"Captain Shannon may blow this one out of the water," Quist said. "Being local, he may think I'm attacking another Mr. Wonderful."

"Someone local?" Shannon asked.

"Howard Seaton," Quist said.

"He wasn't even here," Shannon said. "He was in Ohio."

"The husband of the lady Lewis was with after the party?" Sloan asked.

Quist nodded. "Listening to you talk, he becomes a possibility to me," he said. "Larry has been in residence here at Rainbow Hill, off and on, for several months, getting it ready. Right? He met Madge Seaton when he first came here to look at the property with an eye to buying it, right? If he was having an affair with her, it could have started quite a while ago. Seaton was in Ohio, building his golf course, only back here every week or ten days. Small town, the affair between Larry and Madge Seaton could have been local gossip, right? Howard Seaton is tipped off by some gossipy neighbor. He could have decided this fancy movie star who was tampering with his marriage should be punished. He could have known everything that was going on here at the Inn—the swimming pool's enlargement being postponed. He could have talked to workmen, local friends, and learned that the dynamite was locked away in the toolshed. He flies in and out in his own plane. He could have come back some night to some other airport, got into town without his wife knowing it, and planted the dynamite around the cottage—a week, two weeks ahead of time. He was going to blast Larry at a moment of celebration."

"But he would have to have been here last night," Shannon said. "He had to be here to push down the plunger on the detonator that would set off the blast. He wasn't here. He didn't get here until long after the explosion."

"He says. He flies into the local airport at eleven in the morning, just arriving from Ohio—he says. He could have been here earlier, landing, I suggest, at some other airport some distance away, come here to set off the blast when the time came, gone back to his plane, and flown in here later, saying he's just arrived from Ohio. Have you checked out on the Ohio end, Shannon, to find out when he was there, when he wasn't there, when he left for this last trip east?"

Shannon's face was darkened by a scowl. "I just took it for granted," he said. "He seemed satisfied that Lewis just occupied the guest room at his house."

"You questioned him?"

"Just a little while ago, here," Shannon said. "He and Madge, arm in arm, no tensions. I just don't buy it, Quist."

"But it would be worth checking out on him on the other end, wouldn't it?" Sloan said.

"Why would he attack Patti Payne?" Shannon asked. "She hadn't done him any harm."

"There's one possible explanation for that," Quist said. "Patti might have seen him out in the garden, after the party was over and before the explosion. It was dawn. This afternoon she sees him here with his wife to be questioned. She remembers, then, that she saw him at the critical time. She must have reacted in some way, and he tracked her down and killed her."

"It's no wilder than any other theory," Martin said. "Quist is right. Our top priority is to find Larry Lewis, dead or alive. Either way, that will put us on the right track."

"So we get every able-bodied man, woman, and child in town to start combing the countryside," Sloan said. "It's a needle-in-a-haystack job, but the needle is there, some-where." They all started to move out, but Quist wasn't through. "What are you doing about protecting Miss Ames and Miss Jadwin?" he asked.

"I have a trooper assigned to each of them," Shannon said.

"I was wondering if there was a room somewhere they could share," Quist said. "They might feel safer together than each in her own quarters. They'd be easier to guard that way, too." He was looking at Bobby Crown.

"There's a double room and bath on the second floor," Bobby said. "The Renshaws had it, but they've been allowed to go home. I assume it's been remade, but God knows who's doing their proper job today."

"Arrange it, Bobby, and I'll tell them."

Sandra and Bev had emerged from the card room and were still in the lobby, surrounded by two friends and a couple of reporters. Quist took them aside and told them what he'd arranged.

"Oh, we'll be all right where we are," Bev said.

"It's going to be a long night, with a killer creeping around somewhere," Quist said. "An hour from now, you may be grateful for each other's company. And it'll be easier to guard you if you're both in one place."

"You really think we're in danger?" Bev asked.

"I don't think we can afford to take the risk that you're not," Quist said.

The two women headed for their rooms to collect what they needed for the night, each accompanied by a trooper. Quist headed upstairs to the second floor, where Bobby was checking out the double room with the floor maid. The routine job of preparing the room for the next guest had been done.

"Were you on duty here this morning?" Quist asked the maid.

"This is Nora Wade," Bobby said. "Local girl."

"No, sir," the girl said. She looked a little frightened. "I'm on the night shift—but I was here early this morning. I guess the explosion woke the whole town. As soon as we knew where it was, everyone rushed here, especially those of us who work here."

"And you went home later?"

Nora shook her head. "I haven't been home at all. Betsy Evans, the girl who works this floor on the day shift, was pretty shaken up. Who wasn't? I stayed here to keep her company, and help if it was needed."

"Were you on this floor when Miss Payne came up here in the afternoon?"

The girl's lips trembled. "There's a linen room at the end of the hall with a couple of chairs and a table where the maid on duty can make herself comfortable. We have a Mr. Coffee machine there and a TV set. By afternoon Betsy and I were anchored there, watching what came on the news broadcasts. We must have been watching it when—when it happened. Oh my God! If—if she screamed for help, we didn't hear it. There's a signal box in the room. If a guest wants something, they just press a button in their room and the maid goes to see what they want. Poor Miss Payne never got to the button that would have called us. We were sitting there, only a few yards away, when somebody killed her."

"So you didn't see anyone coming or going from her room?"

The girl's voice was husky. "We were watching the TV."

"In the morning, as soon as the guests leave their rooms, the maid remakes the bed, cleans up generally. By afternoon their routine job is done," Bobby Crown explained, looking down at his feet as he spoke. "No reason for them to be watching for anything in the afternoon, just wait in their place for a call in case a guest wants something."

"Don't get me wrong," Quist said to the girl. "I'm not suggesting that you did something wrong. There was just a chance you might have seen someone."

"Everyone cleared out of here so soon after the explosion," Nora said. "Packed their bags and went downstairs, hoping to get away when the cops would let them. Betsy and I were sure none of them would be coming back, so we made up the beds all fresh, new towels in the bathrooms, ready for the next person who might be going to use the room—if there ever would be anyone!"

"Thanks for checking this out now," Quist said. "I'll wait for the ladies." He turned to Bobby. "You better get some rest, friend. You're going to pass out on your feet if you don't."

Quist walked over to the windows. They looked down on the garden. The police had set up some kind of searchlight down there, focused on the ruins of the cottage. Several men were poking around in the still-smoking rubble, looking for who knows what—anything that might help.

Sandra was the first one to arrive, carrying an overnight bag, her trooper right behind her.

"I'm glad you're here, Julian," she said. "I didn't think

this was necessary when you first suggested it, but while I was packing my things I began to be very glad it was happening. Do the police have any real idea who—?"

Quist shook his head. "An ex-lover of Glenda's driven by jealousy, an unknown enemy of Larry's, Larry himself—"

"Oh, no!"

"The husband of the lady where Larry spent the night after the party, and Mr. X."

"Mr. X?"

"Someone who hasn't surfaced yet."

"Why are Bev and I supposed to be in danger?"

"If it was Glenda's ex-lover, he wants to wipe out Larry and everyone close to him. If it was an unknown enemy of Larry's, same motive. If it was Larry, he invited his four ex-wives here to wipe them all out."

"You don't believe that for a minute, do you?"

"I don't lean that way," Quist said. "If it was Howard Seaton, the husband of Larry's local love life, he just wanted to destroy everyone close to Larry. Mr. X and the unknown enemy are really one and the same. He's tasted blood and he may want some more, especially from people Larry cared about."

"Just none of it makes sense!"

"And I doubt if it will when we find the answer," Quist said. "Because it doesn't and probably won't make sense, we can't take chances. Not with you and Bev."

At which point Bev appeared, followed by her trooper and two bellboys carrying bags, some dresses on hangers. She was ready, Quist thought, to spend a month in the country, not just one night at a party.

The two troopers, after a whispered conversation, went over to the windows. It was obvious that they were looking for a fire escape that could act as a way in from the outside. There was none.

"No vines or a tree you could use to climb up," the

trooper whom Martin had called Toby said. "How do you get out of here in case there's a fire on the other side of the door?"

Quist pointed to a coiled-up rope ladder, neatly packed and placed just by a radiator that was at the window. There was one in his room, carefully pointed out to him by the bellboy who'd brought him up when he'd arrived.

"All the comforts of home," the other trooper said. He turned to Bev. "My name is Watson, Miss Jadwin. Toby and I will station ourselves just outside the door in the hall. If you want something or if you decide you want to go somewhere, let us know and give us time to figure out how to plan it."

The two troopers went out, closing the door behind them.

"Those two clucks don't fill me with confidence," Bev said. "They're supposed to be protecting us from a madman, and they leave us alone here with a man they don't know."

"Meaning me?" Quist asked.

"Meaning you," Bev said. "Don't get me wrong, Julian. I'm not afraid of you, but how do those two stonefaces know we'll be safe with you?"

"It's my irresistible charm and open face," Quist said.

"So be charming!" Bev said. "After this horror day, we need charm. Why don't they let us go home, Julian? I'd certainly feel safer back in my own apartment in New York."

"But would you be if some lunatic is out to get Larry's ex-women? Here, at least, you have those two 'stonefaces' ready to protect you."

"But why are they keeping us here?" Sandra asked. She'd unpacked her bag, hung last night's party dress in the closet, distributed some toilet articles on the bureau. "It's not just to protect us, is it?"

"I think not," Quist said. "This has been one of the longest days I can remember, from the time the bomb went off this morning, to finding Patti this afternoon, until now. But it's been hectic beyond belief for the police. First the bomb, and who was killed in the cottage? Then Larry disappears after he's helped with that question. An intense search for him, because he could have been the intended target. Then Patti, and a whole new murder case. They haven't been able to find the time to get really started on any direct line of investigation."

"How are we supposed to help with that?" Bev asked. "We've told them everything we know, which is nothing."

"They haven't asked you the right questions," Quist said. "You and Sandra, and Bobby Crown, and possibly Mr. Ricardo, are sort of walking computers on the subject of Larry Lewis. You know all there is to know about his past, his present. Press the right button, and you should come up with an answer that will start things rolling. I think they've worn Bobby right down to the bone, working on him, without the hoped-for result. Your turns may come next. Then there's my partner, Dan Garvey, who's been a close friend in a whole other world than show business, the world of sports. Shannon and the others have reason to hope that the right question will produce an answer that will help them to take off."

"Patti must have been ready to come up with that kind of answer and she was silenced," Sandra said.

The lines around Quist's eyes narrowed. "Half an hour before Patti was killed she hadn't come up with that answer," he said. "She'd been talking to me, she'd been talking to you, and she hadn't come up with anything. Half an hour later she was butchered alive!"

"But how does that affect us?" Sandra asked.

"The missing answer might surface in one of your memories, as it did in Patti's," Quist said. "How safe would you be

106

if the murderer is as close by as he was in Patti's case?"

The phone on the bedside table rang and Sandra, after a nervous glance at the others, answered it. She looked relieved. "Captain Shannon for you, Julian," she said.

"Your friend Garvey is back here," Shannon said when Quist answered. "He'd like you to be present when he tells us what he has."

"On my way." Quist turned to the women and explained.

"I never thought I'd ask you to spend the night in my bedroom—without the usual motives," Bev Jadwin said. "You've scared the hell out of me, but I think we'd feel safer if you were here."

"I'll just be on the other end of the phone in the main office," Quist said.

Seeing Garvey with Captain Shannon and Andrew Martin was somehow like coming out of a fantasy world, a dream sequence, into reality. Dan was solid, real, dependable. There were never any doubts about who he was or what he stood for. After a day of suspecting everyone and their motives, Dan was like a breath of fresh air.

"I'm afraid I sent you on a wild goose chase, chum," Quist said. "Gambling and drugs! The way the wheels are spinning here, you come up with a new 'almost for sure' theory every half-hour."

The squeeze Dan gave his upper arm was reassuringly firm. "Proving something isn't so can be just as valuable as proving that something is," Dan said. "The gambling thing I was sure of, but my contacts in Reno and in the sports world, where Larry surely would have done some big betting if he was so inclined, all came up negative. 'Five-buck Larry,' they called him. Nobody could ever persuade him to put some real cash on the line to back up some conviction about something One old-timer told me he guessed they were all lucky that Larry's limit was a five-spot—

because he won ninety percent of the casual bets he made."

"That seems to take care of that," Martin said.

"Not thorough, but consistent enough to convince me," Garvey said. "As for drugs—well, I've only had a few hours. You understand, everybody in the world is talking about Larry today and what's happened here at Rainbow Hill. People will talk about his betting, about his cavalcade of women, but if there are drugs involved, not many people who know would be likely to talk. But I talked to someone I know in the narcotics division of the New York police. They have nothing on Larry, hadn't heard any rumors about him. My friend got in touch with Hollywood police and Reno. Not a whisper about Larry and drugs." Garvey's face darkened with a kind of sympathy. "I understand you're the one who discovered Patti Payne had been murdered. Rough."

Quist nodded.

"Coming on someone dead you've seen alive and well only a little while ago is hard to take," Garvey said. "I was driving from Yankee Stadium downtown after a game some years ago. My closest friend on the team—Jim Rivers, you remember him?—had left a little ahead of me. We'd been horsing around, making plans for the evening. We'd won a tough game, and we were going to do a little celebrating. I came on a wreck on the Major Deegan, just before the Triboro Bridge. Car smashed to pieces, burning. The police were dragging the driver out of the car, badly smashed up, his hair on fire. It was Jim. I never want to go through anything like that again." Garvey gave his shoulders a shake as though the memory still gave him pain. "But while I've spent most of my time disproving your theory about some kind of mob revenge, Julian, I've come up with some other tidbits."

"Take your time, of course," Andrew Martin said sourly. His veneer of good humor was wearing thin.

"I thought I'd try to check out on this guy McNally," Dan said. "Garage in town where I keep my car just happens, by luck, to be the place where Fred Forrest keeps his cars. They know McNally there. I got onto his family, a wife, a couple of kids. They were already in mourning."

"It's been on TV, of course," Shannon said. "Forrest's suggestion that McNally was killed in a rescue attempt."

"Which is what he might say to cover his daughter's reputation," Dan said "But McNally's wife, a former showgirl, believes it. I asked her where he might go if he had escaped it and might be safe. Then it came out. She and McNally have been separated for about a year. He's got a one-room apartment right around the corner from the garage. But if he was alive, not hurt, he'd have been in touch. He would never want the two kids—two nice little boys about eight and ten—to suffer through thinking their father was dead if he wasn't. Whatever his problems were with his wife, McNally, she says, was a devoted father."

"And sleeping with an heiress," Martin said.

"Which brings me back to my theory that Glenda Forrest was the target," Shannon said.

"Planned for well ahead, before even Glenda knew she was going to be in the cottage?" Martin asked.

"Just so we keep juggling as many balls as possible," Shannon said, obviously angry, "I have to give Mr. Quist a score. Howard Seaton keeps his plane at an airport in Cleveland. He was cleared for takeoff out there at nine o'clock last night. It takes a jet airliner about an hour and forty-fifty minutes to fly from Cleveland to New York. It would probably take a little two-seater like Seaton's something over two hours. That means if he'd flown directly to Rainbow Hill, as is his custom, he should have arrived here not later than eleven-thirty. He didn't show up here, publicly, till almost twleve hours after that. He could have landed at some neighboring town, come here to set up the blast while the party was in full swing, pushed the plunger on the detonator at six-forty-five in the morning, taken off to where he'd left his plane, and apparently arrived here about eleven in the morning. An alibi that isn't an alibi."

"So why aren't you talking to him?" Quist asked.

"I've sent a trooper to get him," Shannon said. "He should be here any minute."

The Seatons, Madge and Howard, did arrive moments later, accompanied by the trooper who'd been sent to fetch them. Madge Seaton was clinging, almost desperately, to her husband's arm, as if she expected someone to drag her away from him. Seaton looked undisturbed.

"I assume you haven't found Larry Lewis," he said to Shannon, "and you think Madge can give you some sort of lead as to where he might be. She's told you everything she knows, Captain."

"Can we review what she has told us?" Shannon said.

"Well, she explained to you how Lewis—"

"Let Mrs. Seaton tell us," Shannon said.

If anything, Madge Seaton seemed to press tighter against her husband. "Larry knew what the party was going to be like," she said. "He knew he'd be surrounded for hours by friends and the press. He asked me—I guess the day before—if he could disappear into our guest room when the party ended so that he could get some rest."

"You agreed to offering him that hospitality?"

"Of course. Larry was a friend and a valued customer of Seaton Real Estate."

"You were on a first-name basis with him?"

Seaton laughed. "Naturally she was on a first-name basis with him, we both were, Captain. Hell, he was back and forth for six or eight months setting up the deal for the Rainbow Hill property; another six months after that overseeing the new decorations, furnishings, recruiting a local crew to operate the place. Madge was with him every step of the way. She wouldn't call him 'Mister' after months of that, would she?"

"Your relationship with Larry Lewis was purely business, Mrs. Seaton?" Shannon asked.

"Business at first," Seaton said "Business and friendship later. Larry was easy to like."

"Please let Madge answer the questions, Seaton," Shannon said. "This is a small town, Madge. There have been rumors for some time now that your relationship with Larry Lewis was something more than a business association, or just friendship. Any justification for those rumors?"

Seaton's face hardened. "Let me ask you something, Shannon. Are we charged with something? Is this an official interrogation?"

"Everything connected with this case is official," Shannon said. "We called you in to ask you for help. If you don't want to give it, call in your lawyer and we'll charge you."

"With what?"

"Suspicion of murder," Shannon said.

"Which one?" Seaton asked. "Because since I got here this morning, Madge and I haven't been alone for five minutes—friends, reporters. Neither Madge nor I could possibly have had anything to do with the Payne woman's murder. We're alibied up to our ears. As for blowing up the cottage, I wasn't even here. Do you suspect Madge of that?"

"Where were you, Howard?" Shannon asked. "Where were you when the cottage was blasted?"

"You probably know I'm designing and supervising the building of a new golf course outside of Cleveland, Ohio," Seaton said.

"But you weren't there last night," Shannon said. "You left Cleveland at nine o'clock last night. You could have been here by eleven-thirty. But you didn't make an appearance until almost twelve hours after that. How did you use those twelve hours, Howard?"

Seaton's smile did not reflect amusement. "You've been a busy little bee, haven't you, Shannon? Yes, I left Cleveland at nine o'clock. I thought I'd surprise Madge by turning up at the party."

"Surprise her in bed with Lewis?" Andrew Martin asked.

"You keep your filthy mouth shut, Martin," Seaton said. "I developed engine trouble on the flight east. I put down at a little airfield near Pittsfield, Massachusetts. I had to locate a mechanic who could repair my engine. The only man qualified to do the job wasn't available. Ironically, he was here in Rainbow Hill. A lot of private planes coming in for the party; they'd needed extra help. The Pittsfield guy had been hired to be here for the night."

"So?"

"So I took a room at a motel near the Pittsfield airport. Oh, it'll check out, Shannon."

"You didn't let your wife know where you were?"

"It was midnight by the time I knew I couldn't keep traveling," Seaton said. "The party would be in full swing, no easy way to contact Madge. Since I'd planned to surprise her, she wasn't expecting me, so where I was didn't matter. I slept in the motel. It wasn't until I got up about eight o'clock that I heard the news about what had happened here. I tried to call Madge then, but there was no answer. I assumed that she, and probably everyone else in town, was up here at the Inn. I got my plane fixed and got here as quickly as I could. You can look skeptical, Shannon, but every damn word of it will check out."

"Pittsfield is only about an hour's drive from here," Shannon said. "You could have rented a car, borrowed one, or hitchhiked—been here to set off the blast—and gone back."

"I could also have been on a rocket to the moon and back," Seaton said. "What, by the way, is supposed to be my motive for blowing up the cottage?"

"Your wife was having an affair with Larry Lewis," Shannon said in a flat voice. "You expected him to be in the cottage."

A nerve twitched along the line of Seaton's jaw. "And I stole the dynamite, planted it, and set it off with a couple of hundred people milling around?"

"You could have planted the charge the last time you were home," Shannon said. "All you had to do this time was set it off."

"Oh, boy!" Seaton said. He held out his hands in front of him. "So put the cuffs on me, Captain. It will make a hero out of you until my lawyer has made hamburger out of you."

Shannon glanced at the county attorney and the homicide trooper. Should he or shouldn't he?

"Would it be out of order for me to ask Mrs. Seaton a question or two?" Quist asked in a quiet voice.

"I don't see what right you have to—" Seaton began.

"Larry Lewis is my friend," Quist interrupted. "He is your friend—or is he? If he is, then you must be as concerned as I am about what may have happened to him. Perhaps if we pooled what we know it would help find him."

Madge Seaton looked up at her husband. "It's all right, Howie," she said.

"Till I say stop," Seaton said.

"Let me say, to start with, that I know how easy it would be for small-town gossip to start about any woman who had any kind of close relationship to Larry," Quist said. "There's his reputation with women, to start with. It's part of his glamor image as a big star. Then there's his manner, an embrace and kiss when you meet—in public. It's part of the show-business world. Everybody is 'darling.' In my world, you don't even notice. In a small town like this, people hope it's all sinister. Scandal delights them, and so they spread the word. It's not based on anything real, just on what they hope is real."

"You seem to read this town pretty well," Seaton said. "I've had half a dozen hints that Madge and Larry were an item. I just laughed it off."

"You couldn't spend the better part of a year in a business-friendship relationship with Larry without his being flirtatious, making suggestive remarks in public. It's his way. But he must have thought of you as a real friend, Mrs. Seaton, or he wouldn't have asked for shelter at your house after the party."

Madge nodded, not looking at Quist. He guessed that she was afraid if she did, he would read the truth. Larry had said he'd 'spent the night in the lady's bed.' That, Quist thought, was the truth. "You say Larry asked you the day before the party if he could go to your place when the party was over?"

Madge just nodded again.

"That was before he knew that Glenda was going to ask him for the use of the cottage," Quist said. "Did he give you a special reason, Mrs. Seaton?"

She moistened her lips. "He just said that when the party was over people wouldn't let it be over if he was still available," she said. "He knew he was going to be pretty exhausted. Not much sleep the night before, getting ready. None that night unless he could get away somewhere."

"He must have talked to you about the party in advance," Quist said. "Inviting his four ex-wives—did he talk about that?"

"Yes." Madge hesitated. "I—I thought it was strange. I mean, all four of them being willing, the talk there was sure to be about it. He asked why else I thought he was doing it. Opening the Inn was just a business venture. No one would particularly care. But a party starring four ex-wives—" She glanced across the room at Dan Garvey, who'd remained silent through all of this. "I wasn't sure whether it was Larry's idea or Mr. Garvey's. But it certainly attracted attention."

"It was Larry's idea," Garvey said. "I had to agree it was a sensational way to publicize the opening."

"Did Larry indicate he had any trouble getting the ladies to agree?" Quist asked Madge Seaton.

"He said they were his friends. They'd play along with him." She nodded, slowly. "He did say Mr. Forrest, Glenda's father, would probably whip up a storm when he heard about it. I believe he wangled an invitation for one of his men. Larry said he would point him out to me at the party, but neither he nor Glenda ever appeared."

"Paul Powers," Shannon said.

"Anyone else who might make trouble?" Quist asked. "All of the ladies have had other men interested in them who might have resented the whole idea."

"He didn't mention anyone but Glenda's father and the man who managed to get invited. Larry had to invite the man, this Powers, or Glenda couldn't have made it. Unless all four of the ex-wives put in an appearance, it wouldn't have worked as a publicity stunt."

"There's one other angle I'd like to ask you about, Madge," Quist said. "You helped Larry to pick people to work here."

"Right from the start," Madge said. "I mean, this is my town. I knew the building contractors, painters, plumbers—everyone he needed. I spread the word about his need for maids and maintenance men, college kids he could use for bellboys and that kind of thing. You could say I got him everyone he needed, directly and indirectly."

"So who did he have a row with?"

"No one—that I know of. He took my word about people." She looked up at her husband. "Howie helped, too."

"He was a good man to work for," Seaton said. "He said

what he wanted, and he didn't keep looking over anyone's shoulder. When the job was done, he said thanks, and that was that."

"Mr. Wonderful!" Andrew Martin muttered.

"No grudges, no sour talk about him locally?" Quist asked.

"I—I never heard any, relating to the Inn or to the jobs and the work here," Madge said.

"Relating to anything else?"

Howard Seaton put his arm around his wife in a loving embrace. "People suggested the local ladies should be locked away from him. Ladykiller."

"But you didn't lock your lady away?" Captain Shannon asked.

"Why should I? I trusted her. Larry meant a lot in commissions to us. I understood his style, which Quist has described. When you trust, you trust. It's as simple as that." And then, when no one spoke, "If you're going to bring charges against me, Shannon, get on with it. If not, we'd like to go home."

There was a wordless checkout between Shannon, Martin, and Sloan.

"You can go, Howard," Shannon said. "But don't leave town till I've checked out your story in Pittsfield."

As the Seatons left, the three men put their heads together and Quist found himself standing alone with Garvey.

"The lady is lying in her beautiful white teeth," Garvey said.

"About her relationship with Larry, probably," Quist said. "About the rest, I think not. We still haven't got hold of the right handle on this mess, Dan."

"You think the husband's story will hold up?"

"If I was a big gambler, like Larry, I'd bet five bucks it does," Quist said.

"So what's next?"

"Patti Payne knew something and was silenced to keep

her from telling us. Larry hasn't lived a secret life. Maybe someone else knows what Patti knew and will remember. Let's hope we get a lead to this monster before that happens."

"The other two wives?" Garvey suggested.

"That's where I'm headed," Quist said. "They're together, scared out of their wits, and I don't have anything that will reassure them."

"Larry has the answer if he's alive," Garvey said. "I'll check out on the search parties. I'll see you later."

Garvey was just starting for the door when the huddle among the three law men broke up.

"Talk to you two gents for a little before you take off?" Captain Shannon asked.

"Why not?" Garvey said.

"Officer Sloan thinks you might be helpful." Shannon turned to the dark-faced homicide man.

"You two are personal friends of Larry Lewis's in addition to handling his public relations?" Sloan asked.

"Dan is a great deal closer friend than I am," Quist said. "Our firm is handling his PR work."

"As you both know," Sloan said, "we're going round and round in circles until we're all dizzy. First this one was the target, now that one was the target; the dead man in the cottage was in bed with the lady, or he was trying to rescue her. Larry Lewis is gone because the killer meant to get him and has taken a second shot at him, or the killer has punished him for being a party to the lady's sleeping with the wrong guy. And on and on. Now we have a second murder, with all the indications that the Payne woman knew something and might have been about to tell it, or this is some kind of a diabolical plot to wipe out Lewis and his ex-wives, which means there are still two to go." Sloan made an impatient gesture. "So you pays your money and you takes your choice."

"You've left out the man who had engine trouble, whose

117

wife was carrying on with Larry," Garvey said. "You evidently go along with Julian, who thinks Seaton's story will prove out."

"Fasten your seat belts, friends," Andrew Martin said. "Sloan is about to explode the myth of Mr. Wonderful."

"Let's look at what we have," Officer Sloan said. "The point has been made, over and over, that Larry Lewis can't go ten feet without being recognized. Everyone knows him by sight, he couldn't disguise himself even by wearing a false face. He's a little guy with a dancer's body. Since everybody is looking for him, it would be a miracle if a little guy, no matter how well disguised, could go unquestioned if he showed up in public."

"So the killer got him and has disposed of the body," Garvey said.

"He was walking around here in broad daylight after the explosion, after Captain Shannon took over," Sloan said. "He helped identify who was in the cottage, explained where he'd been when the cottage blew up."

"And that proves out," Garvey said. "Madge Seaton backs up that story."

"Then he just disappears into the wild blue yonder," the homicide officer said.

"The killer caught up with him somewhere, stuck a gun in his ribs, and told him to walk," Quist said.

"And took him where?" Sloan asked. "He didn't leave in a car, his or somebody else's. No car has left here that wasn't checked out, had a clearance from Captain Shannon."

"Locked up in a trunk, dead or bound and gagged," Garvey said.

"Locked up in a car trunk with hundreds of people milling around watching every move that anyone made? It was daytime, not night."

"Everyone was celebrating the fact that he was here, alive, that he hadn't been in the cottage," Quist said. "He could go where he pleased and no one would have given it a thought. Whoever was with him was a friend. Everyone here at Rainbow Hill was a friend. If that 'friend' had a gun in his ribs, Larry would have acted it out if he thought that was his best chance."

"But after he disappears, no one reports having seen him going anywhere with a 'friend,'" Sloan said.

"Get to where you're going," Garvey said, his face turned hard.

"There was no friend," Sloan said. "There was no gun in his ribs. Larry Lewis is the killer."

"Oh, brother!" Quist said.

"So that's impossible?" Sloan said. "So he's Mr. Wonderful. But let's look at it without that myth getting in the way. To begin with, he knows every inch of this property better than anyone else, every service entrance, every back corridor, every storage room or space. He would know how to get anywhere on this property without being obvious. He knew where the dynamite was stored, discussed it with Bobby Crown, joked about it. He could have set up the explosion at the cottage days ahead of time, some night when there was no one around at all. The Inn wasn't open until yesterday when the guests arrived for the party."

"He didn't know that Glenda was going to occupy the cottage that far ahead," Quist said. "She hadn't asked him till yesterday afternoon."

"If she hadn't asked him, he'd have offered it," Sloan said.

"Everything you say could be so," Garvey said. "But why? Why would he plan to kill Glenda in such a flamboyant fashion?"

"That's what I wanted to ask you," Sloan said.

"Wrong computer," Garvey said. "There is no explanation that goes with that."

"He's a man in his sixties," Sloan said, "top of the heap, no place further to go up. Something can happen to a man when he reaches that point in a long life, a screw comes loose. Certain resentments have piled up, and he starts to chew on them with an unbalanced mind."

"What kind of resentments?" Quist asked.

"Vanities, for one thing," Sloan suggested. "Here's a woman he lost who's sleeping around with everyone else. Rubs it in by asking for his help. That woman, in bed with another man in his cottage, spotlights a failure. All four of those ex-wives represent failures, don't they?"

"I don't think so," Garvey said. "They were people with whom he'd shared an intimacy who remained friends when that close period ended."

"Maybe that was so, for many years," Sloan said, "but now that screw has come loose and we're talking about a psycho."

"So he invites them all here to kill them?" Quist asked. "Honestly, Sloan, are you sure *you* haven't got a screw loose somewhere?"

"Money is no problem with this man," Sloan said, sounding stubborn. "He buys a million-dollar property; he plans a grand opening, he hires you to publicize the fact that his four ex-wives are to be his honored guests. Theatricality is the name of his game. He kills the four women who demonstrate that he was a failure, and nobody dreams of pointing at him because he's Mr. Wonderful. He will act out his grief when the time comes."

"And where was he after the explosion and his return from the Seatons'? Where was he when Patti was killed? Where will he have been when the other two get theirs?" Garvey asked.

"Maybe he'll be crazy enough to admit it when it's all done. Show the world that Mr. Wonderful can wipe out his failures in a dramatic fashion."

"This is all wildly fascinating, Sloan," Quist said, "but I think I'll keep on trying to find Larry."

"Before you do, know that we've been over every square inch of this plant. Bobby Crown probably knows it as thoroughly as his boss. Outside, in the surrounding country-side, some expert woodsmen along with scores of volunteer helpers plus some well-trained dogs have been over hundreds of acres. They're going back over that same territory again right now, just in case." Sloan's voice was stern. "You and Garvey can be a lot more helpful telling what you really know about Larry Lewis."

"It won't make much difference what we tell you if Larry's blown his stack, will it?" Garvey asked. "You've already invented a motive for a Larry Lewis with a loose screw."

"If, by some farfetched piece of luck, you should be right," Quist said, "then the most important thing is to find Larry, before he can do any more damage."

"Was he jealous of his women when he was married to them?" Sloan asked, ignoring both comments.

"You know him better than I do," Quist said to Garvey.

"I've known him for twenty years, and I don't think he's spoken ten sentences to me about the women in his life," Garvey said. "He was a sports nut, I was part of the sports world. I can tell you exactly what he thought of Mickey Mantle or Y. A. Tittle, but not about women. We weren't interested in the same women, so we had nothing to share. So now, for God's sake, let's try to find him. If you should be wrong, Sloan, there's just a chance we could still save him from the real killer."

"It could be, you know," Garvey said, as he and Quist walked out into the Inn's lobby. "I mean, you passionately defend a man you know, a friend, and you think how absurd it is to imagine he could become a mass murderer. But if something does snap in his head, if a screw does come loose, then he's no longer the man you know. You're defending someone who no longer exists, a stranger walking around in an old familiar body."

"So that anything you, or I, or the two remaining ex-wives, or Bobby Crown, or any good friend knows about Larry simply does not apply to whoever is walking around in Larry's skin," Quist said. "There are other things that may not add up."

"Such as?"

"They've searched the Inn from top to bottom, over and over. No Larry. Trained people and dogs have searched the woods and are searching them over again. No Larry. Doesn't that tell us something, Dan? That they're looking in the wrong place?

Garvey nodded. "He couldn't have been carried away from here in a car. They were searched and checked out. But he *was* carried away in a car. Somebody slipped up."

"The question is, did he go voluntarily or did he go at the point of a pistol?" Garvey asked.

They were standing at the foot of the stairs leading up from the lobby to the second floor, where Sandra Ames and Bev Jadwin were being guarded by their two troopers. Quist brought his fist down hard on the newel post.

"Why would he go anywhere voluntarily? He was safe here, his friends were here, the cops were here."

"Screw loose," Garvey said.

"So we're back to that. I promised to check in with Sandra and Bev. Come with me?"

The two troopers assigned to guard the two ex-wives had found chairs and were sitting in them directly outside the door of the suite.

"I'd like to go back in," Quist said. "This is Dan Garvey, my partner."

"Have to give you a weapons search," the trooper named Toby said.

"You looking for a carving knife?" Garvey asked.

"Wouldn't you?" the trooper said.

The body search was quick. The trooper knocked on the door and Sandra's voice answered.

"Mr. Quist and Mr. Garvey to see you, Miss Ames," the trooper said. "You want us to let them in?"

"Please!"

The second trooper unlocked the door from the outside and opened it. Sandra was standing just inside. Bev was sitting at a little coffee table across the room, looking tense, as if she expected the visitors to be anyone but the people announced.

"You've been gone forever," Sandra said to Quist. "Hi, Dan."

"We've been watching the garbage on television till we're ready to throw up," Bev said. "What's really going on? Do they have the faintest idea about Patti?"

"They've got a thousand ideas and no facts," Garvey said. "The latest dream is that Larry has gone crazy and is out to kill you all."

Sandra actually laughed. "I suppose we need jokes so we can relax," she said.

"Larry has either blown a fuse or he is in terrible danger—or he is dead," Quist said. "I can't laugh at any of those possibilities, luv."

"What's funny is that those stupid cops can't find Larry or make an attempt to catch who is after him," Bev said. "They couldn't have done anything to protect Glenda, but Larry was walking around here, alive and well, when he disappeared right under their noses. Patti, poor darling, was surrounded by big, brave cops, and she was butchered. We're in the hands of bungling fools, Julian."

The two men settled in chairs around the little coffee table, and Sandra brought two mugs and a coffeepot from the kitchenette.

"You'll have to take it black the way we do," she said.

"I haven't asked you," Garvey said, after sipping his coffee. "I know you've been asked, but I didn't hear the answer from you. What did Patti know that made the killer so viciously silence her?"

"Nothing that she told either Sandra or me," Bev said.

"There were almost two hundred people milling around here during the party," Garvey said. "You and Sandra and Patti almost certainly knew most of them, or at least who they were and why they might have been on Larry's guest list. You don't come up at once with anyone you might suspect of having it in for Glenda, or Larry, or both. You would have to go over the list, thinking, remembering, trying to guess at someone. It might not happen for hours or days. But in Patti's case, she remembered something between the time she left you gals in the lobby and went up to her room."

"How did the killer know that she had remembered?" Sandra asked.

"Not necessarily that she *had* remembered," Quist said, "but that she almost certainly would."

"You've known Larry for almost forty years, Sandra," Garvey said. "It's too much to expect you to go back over those forty years, day by day, but there must have been quarrels with someone, frustrations that Larry never got over. There must have been people who resented his success, who felt he had done something to undercut them, even though Larry didn't mean to and you didn't think he did. The same holds true of you, Bev. Both of you were very close to Larry for several years, and from what you've said— what I've heard—stayed friends with him long after your period of marital closeness had ended. You can't go hunting the Rainbow Hill plant for Larry, or search the countryside, but you can search your memories for something that hasn't popped up yet."

"Me first?" Sandra said. "Since I was first, before he even knew Bev, or Patti, or Glenda, or Bobby Crown."

"Talk about it," Garvey said. "Don't dig for what we're trying to find, just talk about Larry as though you were being interviewed by someone who wanted to write his biography. Along the way you may stumble on what it is we're after."

Sandra covered her face with her hands for a moment, as though it was difficult to go back so far in time. Then she lowered her hands and looked past the others toward the darkened windows, as though the past were somehow visible there.

"I—I grew up in Hollywood," she said, her voice uncertain as she began. As she went on, it grew steady, almost as though what she was recalling gave her real pleasure. "Both my parents were actors, neither of them ever getting famous, but good enough to work pretty steadily in films. In my teens I got to know some of the famous people of that time, Clark Gable, Henry Fonda, and a lady I dreamed of being like when I grew up, Claudette Colbert. And then— when I was seventeen—I broke the ice myself, getting a small part in a film that starred Larry Lewis. He was twenty-three at the time, but he'd been a famous child actor before that. He was something very special, a marvelous dancer, a brilliant comic. I don't think anyone had any doubt that he was going on to become a very big star. I—I had a small scene with him, and in the rehearsals it wasn't going well. I just couldn't match the kind of fireworks he was sending up opposite me. I expected he'd complain to the director and they'd find someone else to take my place."

"But of course he didn't," Bev said.

The two women smiled at each other as though they shared a secret.

"We were on location, somewhere in Colorado," Sandra said. "Larry suggested I have lunch with him and we talk about the scene. He didn't take me to the company commissary, but drove me somewhere out into the country. He had a picnic luncheon parked in his car. We didn't eat the lunch right away when he selected a picnic spot. He talked about the scene, explained to me that I wasn't reacting to him but was trying to make a moment of my own. We tried it his way, and suddenly it began to work! After we'd tried it two or three times, he suddenly took me in his arms and kissed me. 'You're going to be great!' he told me. I—I really didn't care at the time. That kiss made me his prisoner for life, I thought. I was in love! What I didn't realize was that being in love was what was needed in the scene. He was acting, but I was feeling. That kiss was repeated in rehearsals and in the eventual shooting of the scene, and I was lost."

"But he wasn't acting. He asked you to marry him," Bev said.

Sandra nodded. "He painted a picture of our working together forever. I didn't care about that. I just wanted to be his woman. We didn't wait for the film to be finished. I don't think anyone will believe that we didn't make love until after we were married. 'I want your wedding night to be magic,' he told me, when I indicated I was quite willing not to wait. But that's the way it was, and it was magic when it happened."

"You were probably his first and only virgin," Bev said, sounding a little amused.

"My parents, my friends, all told me I'd made a big mistake. He already had his reputation with women. But I was in heaven." Sandra hesitated a moment. "It didn't work out the way I'd dreamed it would. We didn't get to work together. He had a new film and there was nothing in it for me. But I'd made something for myself in that first film, and I know Larry sold me in a big way to his friends in the business, and I got work. The result was that we were separated a good part of the time. The Hedda Hoppers and the Louella Parsonses hinted that Larry was romancing his current leading lady, but I never believed it. When we were together, it was still magic."

"You were an innocent eighteen-year-old," Bev said.

"I suppose," Sandra said. "Later I had different thoughts about it. When we were together, he wouldn't have looked at another woman. When we were separated—"

"He played the field," Bev said.

"But it came to an end," Garvey said.

"Five years that I wouldn't trade for anything," Sandra said. "But toward the end, a big starring film took Larry to Europe. He was gone for nearly eight months. At the same time, I got my own big break, a starring film of my own. We wrote, but not often. He called me from overseas a few times. The gossip ladies were at work again, hinting at a new romance with a new leading lady." Sandra looked down at her hands. "Her name was Beverly Jadwin."

"Eight months is a longer dry spell than you could ask of most men," Bev said in a flat voice. "He taught me how to react to him."

"I know," Sandra said. "I saw the film when it was finished. That film romance was more than acting."

"You broke up over Bev," Garvey said.

"Yes and no," Sandra said. "Larry came back from Europe. We tried to pick up where we'd left off and it didn't work. I didn't have it for him, and he didn't have it for me. It was just gone. 'Separations like ours just don't work in a marriage,' Larry told me. 'We've run out of gas.' He was sorry. It had been great while it worked. He didn't talk about Bev and I didn't ask him. I thought I knew."

"I didn't marry him until five years later," Bev said. "My story and Sandra's are almost identical. Magic for a few years and then, boom!"

"You resented each other?" Garvey asked.

"That was so long ago," Sandra said. "I suppose we did. But after Larry's marriage to Bev came to an end, we got to be friends, good friends. I guess we needed to share our experiences to try to find out where we had failed."

"And did you?"

"I don't think we did, failed, I mean," Sandra said. "I think the problem was Larry's. He thought he wanted permanence, he tried for it four times, didn't he? But he could only run one course for a limited length of time. It just wasn't in him to stay put forever."

"But you've become friends with him since the break-ups?"

"He came to me when he'd decided to have a go at it with Bev," Sandra said. "No one had ever been as close to him as I had. What had he done wrong with me? What could he do to make sure he didn't fail a second time? He hadn't done anything wrong, to tell the truth. Our lifestyles had been at fault. Career separations had been at fault. He and Bev were working together. If it stayed that way, it shouldn't fail."

"But it didn't stay that way," Bev said. "We did two Broadway musicals together, then a film, then contracts we couldn't refuse got us working separately. And like I said, after that—boom!"

"But you two stayed friends and Larry stayed friends with both of you?"

Sandra nodded. "People used to make small talk about it," she said. "Whenever Larry was in the part of the world where I was working or living, he would come to see me, take me to lunch or dinner or the theater. If Bev was with him, the three of us would go places together."

"It was as if Sandra were a member of his family, and it was the same way later with me, when Patti came into the picture," Bev said.

"I've been waiting for you to get to Patti," Quist said, speaking for the first time.

"The same story, third time around," Bev said. "She came to Sandra and me when Larry had popped the question to her to ask what she could do to make it work. Sandra and I should have been experts on the subject, don't you think?"

128

"I guess we were," Sandra said. "I remember telling Patti she should just enjoy it while it lasted. I told her I didn't think it would last, but I thought she'd be crazy not to drink every drop in the glass until it was empty. Knowing what I know now, that five years is just about the top time for Larry, I'd still advise the next woman to take it while it was there to take."

"It's like a wild roller coaster ride," Bev said. "Fun, scary, exciting, but when the ride is over you just get out of the car and walk away. There's no way to buy a second ticket. Something like that is what we both told Patti."

"I think she may have had the best time of all of us," Sandra said. "She went into it without any illusions about its future."

"And Glenda?" Garvey asked.

"Glenda was not one of my favorite people," Sandra said. "She represented some kind of a challenge to Larry, like a wild horse he wanted to tame and ride. He couldn't. She wouldn't be tamed. I think she married Larry just because she knew it would drive her father up the wall. Bev and Patti and I never quarreled with Larry. He isn't quarrelsome. But with Glenda it was a few months of perpetual war. Larry laughed about it to us—his family. He'd bitten off more than he could chew."

"He was bitter about it?" Garvey asked.

"No way," Bev said. "One night he took all three of us, Sandra and Patti and me, to dinner. He told us 'the ballgame is over.' He said, 'You three made me think I was a combination of Prince Charming and Don Juan. Glenda has convinced me I'm an old man without the right juices for a young woman anymore. I'd love to try it all over with one of you, but the chemistry wouldn't be right the second time around.'"

"Would you if he'd asked you?" Quist asked.

"I wouldn't," Bev said. "I had one husband before him and one after. Marriage isn't my game and I knew it by then. But I'd have been pleasantly flattered."

"I might have," Sandra said, "if I'd thought he was serious. I think Patti might have. He'd been my lover, my husband, and a cherished friend for forty years! If he'd wanted me to stand by him at the end and watch the parade go by, I think I would have. But he didn't want to watch the parade, he wanted to be the grand marshal."

"And he didn't ask any of you?"

"Not me," Sandra said.

"Nor me, and I'm sure not Patti," Bev said.

"Patti remembered something," Quist said. "That's really where we started. Remembered something that would have identified a killer."

"I've been waiting for the cork to pop while we've talked," Bev said. "It hasn't. I don't remember any violent enemies Larry made along the way, do you, Sandra?"

Sandra shook her head slowly. "But is that really what we're looking for?" The question was aimed at Quist and Garvey. "Aren't we looking for someone who hated Glenda? That someone knows Patti could have named him if she thought about it. And Larry could name him."

"But he didn't," Quist said. "He was walking around here alive and well after the cottage blew up. The cork didn't pop for him then."

"He hadn't got around to thinking that Glenda was the target. He thought the explosion had been meant for him, and he couldn't think of anyone who hated him that much. I'd like to bet there isn't anyone. Glenda has played with fire all her life and she finally got burned."

Garvey glanced at Quist. "That's Captain Shannon's theory, and I begin to go along with it," he said.

"What kind of fire, Sandra?" Quist asked.

"Men, all over the map," Bev said before Sandra could answer. "There was one word missing from Glenda's vocabulary. It was 'no.'"

"The Club Madrid was one of her hunting grounds," Quist said. "Ricardo says she took off from there with a different man every night. Larry was one of them."

"Larry saved her from a row with her father," Bev said. "Maybe that earned him three days of fidelity."

"Long enough to hook him and hang him out to dry," Sandra said.

"Sloan, the homicide cop, thinks he couldn't have forgiven her for that," Quist said.

"One thing, Larry isn't a bad loser," Sandra said.

"When did he ever lose?" Quist asked. "I could say that he lost you, Sandra, lost Bev, lost Patti. But you say it wasn't losses, just the way it was for him. He certainly didn't hold grudges against any of you."

"You've heard how he liked to bet—small bets, mostly," Sandra said. "In spite of the rumors, he lost quite often. I never knew him to do anything but laugh good-naturedly when he lost. He wasn't obsessed with winning, he just enjoyed the gamble. He gambled on Glenda and lost. I never heard him say anything ugly about her. He just said he'd 'bet on the wrong horse.' But he never lost in his career. He was always on top, always climbing even higher than that. Professionally he didn't know what it was to lose."

"No enemies along the way in that climb?" Garvey asked.

"Larry is a very special talent," Sandra said. "He didn't make enemies, because he wasn't competing with anyone. He is special, an original, a one of a kind. He didn't make enemies, because no one could go after his special kind of excellence. He didn't have to push anyone aside to get the plays and films he got, because there was no one who could do what he can do so well."

"Bobby Crown says he started out trying to be another Larry Lewis," Quist said.

131

Sandra smiled. "Dear Bobby. I guess he had his problems. He's a little man, certainly not able to compete in your world of football giants, Dan. When he first saw Larry in films, he saw a little guy who had really made it. It gave him hope. He got the job as Larry's stand-in in a film. He very quickly realized that he had no gifts that could ever take him to where Larry was. And Larry, sensing how much that hurt the kid, took him on as part of his staff and made a life for him."

"I don't think Larry could function today without Bobby," Bev said. "The cork hasn't popped for him either. He must have been thinking of his twenty-five years with Larry all day today." She frowned. "He was right in the middle of all of Larry's troubles with Glenda. If anyone could point to someone who might have hated Glenda enough to destroy her, he might be it."

"The poor guy is so exhausted at the moment, he doesn't know which way is up," Quist said. "He's been over and over it with the cops."

"Did Glenda ever become a part of Larry's 'family'?" Garvey asked. "Family, meaning three ex-wives and Bobby Crown. When Larry and Glenda broke up, did she join the club? Did she sit around with you at happy cocktail hours gossiping about whatever there was of interest about your mutual pasts?"

"You sound just a little contemptuous, Dan," Sandra said.

"I suppose everybody who was caught in the San Francisco earthquake must have talked about it when they got together," Bev said.

"So was Glenda a member?" Garvey said. "I find a club of ex-wives a little hard to talk about without sounding surprised. But there is a reason for asking about it. If she was a member of the club, that explains why she was invited to the party. If she wasn't a member, then what was her relationship to Larry?"

"It had to be cordial," Quist said, before either woman could answer. "He invited her to the party, lets his arm be twisted so that Paul Powers gets an invitation, cooperates in supplying her with a love nest—which turned out not to be a favor. Special treatment, wouldn't you say?"

"The black sheep of a family often turns out to be much loved," Sandra said. "Glenda was outrageous in the way she paraded the current man in her life under Larry's nose. He could have been hurt, angry. He wasn't. He'd just laugh, the way you might over the mischief of a precocious child."

"He was old enough to be her father," Quist said.

"Which may explain why he reacted to her like an indulgent parent rather than a frustrated lover," Garvey said. "But it's Glenda who puzzled me. Why would she let herself be a party to a publicity stunt for the opening of Rainbow Hill—four ex-wives all under one roof. I'd have thought she might have told Larry to go fly his kite."

"You aren't interested in why Sandra and Patti and I agreed to be part of it?" Bev asked.

"You are 'family,'" Garvey said, almost impatiently. "You are all show business. Publicity gimmicks are in your blood! Opening the Inn here was like an opening night on Broadway."

"Better than most," Bev said.

"But Glenda—wouldn't she have thought she was being used by a man she'd discarded?"

"I asked myself that same question," Sandra said, "both before the party and after—after all the horrors. Why did Glenda let herself be used? She wasn't what you call 'family' and she wasn't show business. Beforehand, I came up with two answers. One, she would outrage her father by being a part of what he'd call a 'cheap publicity scheme.' That would please our little Glenda. Second, she could float some new dreamboat lover under Larry's nose and for the whole world to see. That would please her."

"Instead, she hid him away in Larry's cottage and got blown up for her pains," Bev said.

"So who was the dreamboat? Her father's chauffeur and strong-arm boy? She didn't go public with that. She ducked the party and took him to the cottage."

"Don't let yourselves get carried away," Quist said. "It's not the man who was in the cottage with Glenda we're after. It's the man who blew them up for being there that we want; the man who later killed Patti because she might have remembered something that would point to him."

"We're not much smarter than the cops, are we?" Bev said.

A sharp knock on the suite's door interrupted. It was the state trooper named Toby.

"Captain Shannon says I can take you over to your original room, if you'd care to go now," he said to Bev.

She stood up. "I left some personal things in the bathroom down there," she explained to Quist and Garvey. "I didn't realize I was coming up here forever. Back in a few minutes." She gave the trooper a dazzling smile. "Thanks, Toby." She was already on a first-name basis with her bodyguard.

Quist and Garvey were left alone with Sandra. She poured more coffee for them.

"Our Bev can still make that young trooper's heart flutter a little," she said. "She makes me feel like the Queen Mother, respected but undesired."

"Give me another time and place, and I'll try to scuttle that idea," Quist said.

"Thanks, darling—not that I believe a word of it," Sandra said.

Garvey put his coffee mug down on the table rather more firmly than it needed. "We're supposed to be covering forty years of your life, Sandra, and we still have about thirty-five to go. A murderer is supposed to show his face along the way. You say Larry had no enemies, no jealous rivals. There are people who just hate other people's success, aren't there?"

"I thought you'd moved around to looking for someone in Glenda's life," Sandra said.

"Part of Glenda's life meshed with Larry's, and your life seems to have meshed with forty years of his. Turn your memory to the time when Glenda came into your life."

"Glenda never really came into my life," Sandra said. She closed her eyes for a moment, as if she were trying to go back in time. "I don't think I'd ever heard of her until the night Larry broke up a row between the Forrests in the Club Madrid. The columnists had that one, how Larry had danced and sung a crowd into shushing the great oil tycoon. It was typical. Larry won arguments by charming people. He'd thrown a party afterward for 'the lady in distress.' I just read about it and laughed. I might even have thought, 'That's my Larry,' although he hadn't been mine for nearly thirty-five years." She hesitated. "I suppose there were people, people who thought Larry was suddenly interested in Glenda because she was, one day, going to come into more money than a computer could count. I knew better than that. Just money didn't matter to him—money that he earned as the great Larry Lewis was a special kind of money. It was a symbol of how good he was at what he did. Other kinds of money didn't mean anything."

"When did you guess that Glenda was more than just a night's adventure?"

"About ten days after they met, he came to see me," Sandra said. "Had I heard about the thing at the Club Madrid? I had. The girl, Glenda, was something! He was, he told me, forty-one years, seven months, and four days older than she was. When he said that, I knew it was serious. I knew I was supposed to say something cheerful, like 'You're only as old as you think you are.' I said it. It

135

didn't do too much good. What did I really think about him marrying the girl? Weren't three failures enough? I asked him. He gave me that pixie grin of his and said, 'But it's so much fun while it lasts!'" Sandra reached for her coffee mug. "I couldn't give him any kind of solid advice. I remembered how it had been with me, like driving along the thruway at high speed, top down, hair blowing in the breeze. Then, suddenly you run out of gas, the car slows down, and you have to pull over to the shoulder of the road. The ride was over, but it hadn't been any less fun because it was done. If that's what he wanted—" She shrugged.

"But you weren't against Glenda as a person?" Garvey asked.

"I wasn't against her then because I didn't know her. I wasn't for her, later, when I got to know her, but it didn't matter then because it was over."

"But you didn't like her then?"

"I didn't like her because she didn't give Larry that brief moment of fun he'd expected."

"Did they have a big wedding—all of Hollywood, all of society?"

Sandra laughed. "They didn't have a big wedding because if they'd tried, Glenda's old man would have bought the church out from under them before they could walk up the aisle. A justice of the peace, a couple of strangers as witnesses. Then the big hoopla when the story broke in the news. Fred Forrest threatening to buy out the film industry so Larry would never work again. Larry doing a tap dance on the steps of the public library to the tune of 'Who's Afraid of the Big Bad Wolf?' Nothing about Larry has ever been very private."

"Sounds like a great start," Garvey said.

"About two weeks later, Larry was knocking on my door again. 'You were right,' he told me. 'I said you were only as old as you think you are.' 'I'm an old dog who can't learn new tricks,' he said. What kind of tricks were required? 'She's like a great actress who, after opening night, doesn't care whether the play runs or not. She's had her rave notices, so on to the next vehicle. "

"Just winning was all that mattered to her?" Garvey asked. "Is that really the way it's been with Larry? Four wives, God knows how many in-betweens."

"It might appear to an outsider to be that way," Sandra said. "But I have to tell you something, Dan. Using Larry's analogy of an actor and a play, I can only tell you that while the play was on, Larry never gave a bad performance. It was so good that it never occurred to me that it was acting at all." She made a little gesture toward the heavens. "The management closed the show, but the performance was great, right down to the final curtain. I think Bev would tell you the same thing, and poor Patti if she could. A failed marriage with Larry isn't something any of us would choose to have done without."

"It's too bad he isn't around to hear that," Quist said. "But what about Glenda? Would she say the same thing, if she could be here to say it?"

Sandra's face clouded. "She gave me a hint of how she felt a month or so after she and Larry split up. Of all the places in the world, it was on a Fifth Avenue bus in New York. I boarded it somewhere near the apartment I had uptown, headed for the only empty seat I saw, and the person sitting next to me by the window was Glenda.

"'Meeting of the Larry Lewis alumnae association,' she said. 'How you endured that colossal ego for five years I'll never know—and all the years since when he ran to you for help and advice.'

"'I never advised him about you,' I said, 'beyond telling him to go after you if that's what he wanted.' Then I got a little nasty. 'I understand you wanted him to become a tap-dancing cowboy.'

"'I wanted him to be a man and not a sideshow freak,'" Glenda said. "That's when I got up, walked to the door of the bus and got off at the next stop."

"That's when you decided she wasn't a nice girl," Garvey said.

"Precisely then."

"But you were still willing to go along with a party featuring her as one of four ex-wives?" Quist said.

Sandra didn't answer for a moment. Then she looked straight at Quist. "Rainbow Hill meant more to Larry than you can guess, Julian. And it was different from all the other challenges in his life. In the past the success or failure of anything he tried, including his marriages, depended on his own performance. It wasn't until he got deep into this that he realized that success here depended on a lot of other people, starting with Mr. Ricardo and Bobby, right down to the waiters, the busboys, the maids, the guy with the lawn mower."

"Same thing with a play, isn't it? You have to get the best from the writer, the director, the musicians in the orchestra pit, the supporting actors, the makeup people, the costume people—and on and on."

"True," Sandra said "but with one difference. In a Broadway show or a film, Larry knew he could, with his own special talents, his performing genius, pull it off even if someone goofed along the way. But he had no special talent for running a vacation resort. He got panicky, started looking for gimmicks to get it off the ground. It was you who suggested exploiting the four ex-wives, wasn't it, Dan?"

"It was Larry's idea, but I went for it when he told me you'd all agreed," Garvey said. "Right about now I wish to God I hadn't."

At that moment the door to the suite burst open and Captain Shannon, Sloan, Martin, and half a dozen troopers charged in. No knock, no 'May I?'

"I want to get you out of here as quickly as I can, Miss Ames, to a safe place," Shannon said.

"Safe—from what?" Sandra asked.

"Beverly Jadwin has been murdered," Sloan said in a cold, flat voice. "A psycho is on the lose and you could be next, Miss Ames."

"But she was guarded!" Sandra said. "She had a trooper with her!"

"And still it happened," Sloan said.

PART FOUR

1

It was almost midnight. Twenty-four hours ago a lively party had been in full swing at Rainbow Hill. Right now it was an ugly corner in a part of hell. Troopers, members of the staff, townspeople were crisscrossing each other, all searching for someone, all in an obvious state of panic.

Quist managed to hang on to Andrew Martin long enough to get the bare bones of the story. The trooper, Toby Swenson, had taken Bev Jadwin down to her original room to collect some things she'd left there.

"According to Toby, he played it perfectly safe," Martin said. "Just because things were as hairy as they were, he took a quick look in the closets, went into the bathroom to make sure there was no one there. All clear. Miss Jadwin, he says, turned on the TV set—couldn't bear to be out of touch with what was cooking. He says she watched for a minute and then collected some things out of the bureau. She had a small extra traveling bag in the closet. Then she went into the bathroom for some toilet articles she said she'd left there. She closed the door and Toby assumed she was going to use the facilities. He waited, watching the TV. When he thought she'd been rather extra long, he switched off the TV and called to her. No answer. He knocked on the bathroom door. No answer. Finally he opened the door— and there she was."

Quist moistened his lips. "Where was she?"

"Almost a replica of Patti Payne," Martin said. "Throat cut, a half-dozen stab wounds in the chest, the tile floor a sea of blood."

"Her tongue?" Quist asked, not recognizing the sound of his own voice.

"Bastard didn't get to that," Martin said. "He must not have had time for any artistic flourishes."

"How did the trooper miss him?"

"He says he didn't."

"Hidden in the shower," Quist suggested, reaching for straws.

"First place he looked, Toby says. Only place anyone could hide in the bathroom, so he looked there first."

"How did he get there?"

"A lot of geniuses are trying to figure that one out. The best guess so far is one of those rope fire-escape ladders from the floor above. There's one in every room."

"Who was in the room above Bev's?"

"Empty. Vacated earlier in the day. Excuse me, Quist, but I've got to go somewhere and look as if I knew what I was doing."

"Where is a safe place for Miss Ames?" Quist asked.

Martin's smile was twisted. "Only place I can suggest is Shannon's hip pocket."

Four murders, possibly five if that was what had happened to Larry Lewis, in the space of less than twenty-four hours, was pretty staggering even for the toughest cop to take. For Quist, it was tougher. He had known them all except McNally, the chauffeur presumed to have died with Glenda in the cottage. Now three women, plus McNally, were dead, brutally slaughtered, and Larry might be added to the list before the investigation went much further.

The pattern was so clear, Quist thought. Larry and his "family" of ex-wives were on a hit list. These weren't just indiscriminate killings by someone who enjoyed the taste of blood. This was all aimed at a special group. An outsider like himself, Quist thought, had nothing to worry about.

But Sandra Ames was almost certainly on that hit list if the killer could play out his pattern. Quist wondered if even Shannon's hip pocket was a safe enough place to hide her. Her only real chance for saftey was to nail the killer to the barn door before he could strike again.

Almost no one in the town of Rainbow Hill thought of himself as a spectator in the early hours of that next day. They were all cops chasing one robber, all cowboys chasing one Indian. Too many hunters, Quist thought. Shannon and his troopers were almost forced to abandon a criminal investigation in order to control the small army of hysterical do-gooders. Reporters, another army growing by the minute, were demanding facts about this latest horror. Somewhere some genuine police work must be going on, probably in the bloody bathroom where Bev Jadwin had died, possibly in the room above, looking for proof that the killer had come from there, down one of those rope fire-escape ladders. Fingerprints? To compare against what other fingerprints? There had been no chance of any prints in the totally destroyed cottage, and Quist had heard no word of any being found in Patti Payne's room. If there were any in the bathroom where Bev had died, or in the room on the floor above, what would you match them against? Fingerprint everyone who had been at Rainbow Hill in the last thirty-six hours? A long and tedious job, Quist thought, probably taking days to round up everyone again. Meanwhile, Sandra's life was on the line. They could take her to the trooper barracks, lock her in a cell, or send her to a military fortress somewhere and surround her with soldiers. Then, unless they caught and convicted the killer, she would still be in danger when they had to set her free.

Quist had slipped into the card room where he'd been with others before. He wanted a quiet moment to try to decide what his role should be from here on in. He had nothing at this point to contribute to the police except

145

Sandra's and Bev's rambling stories about Larry Lewis and their romances with him. Sensibly he should go to Shannon, explain that he had nothing, and suggest getting out of the captain's hair by leaving Rainbow Hill. One less finger in the pie would have to make things easier for the professionals. Yet Sandra was his friend, a closer friend now than she'd been before the start ot this grisly weekend. She was a gracious, charming, and lovely lady whose basic security for most of her life had been an ex-husband who had remained a good and dependable friend. There must be two thoughts going through Sandra's mind at the moment. Larry was also a victim of this psycho killer and she was without her main security, or, worse than that, Larry had blown his stack and she was waiting to be confronted by the man she still loved, armed with a butcher knife! Heads you lose, tails I win.

If Larry was dead, or if he had a moment of sanity here and there in his homicidal disaster, he would hope that there was someone to stand by Sandra, his first love, his lifelong "family." I am it, Quist told himself. Was he just to sit beside her and wait for the killer's next move, or was he to play detective like everyone else at Rainbow Hill?

The door to the card room opened and Dan Garvey came in.

"Been looking for you," Garvey said. "Shannon's about to let the reporters have a go at Toby Swenson, the trooper who was with Bev. Only way to be let alone to do his job. You're invited—since you and I were the last people to talk to Bev—before it happened."

The lobby was as crowded as it had been at the party, but the faces weren't happy.

"Sandra?" Quist asked as they headed toward the office Shannon had commandeered.

"Her world has caved in on her," Garvey said. "Like an automaton, going where they tell her to go, saying what they tell her to say."

Reporters were jammed together outside the office. A few others, selected by Shannon, were to take part in the interview with Trooper Swenson and pass along what they got to the others. Sandra was there, looking like someone in a trance. Quist wasn't sure that she recognized him when he raised his hand to wave to her.

Toby Swenson was having trouble maintaining his deadpan trooper face. A nerve twitched in his cheek; his lips were stiff as though it were hard for him to shape them to make words. He read a brief statement to the reporters, pretty much what Martin had told Quist. It was as if Swenson needed the paper he held in his not-too-steady hands to remind him of what had happened a relatively short time ago. When he'd finished, Shannon told reporters who had questions to hold up their hands. Everyone raised a hand. Shannon recognized one of them and the questions began.

"To you, Captain Shannon," a reporter said. "If you knew Bev Jadwin was in danger, why did you let her go back to her room?"

"We didn't really know she was in danger," Shannon said. "But we weren't taking chances, so we sent a man with her." He recognized another reporter.

"You searched the room and the bathroom," that reporter said to Swenson. "Did you draw your gun? Were you ready for trouble?"

"To tell you the truth, I didn't expect that kind of trouble," Swenson said. "Miss Jadwin was a theatrical personality. I really thought I might find a fan, waiting for an autograph, or one of you reporters, or a souvenir hunter. There wasn't anyplace to hide in the bedroom except the closet. No one there. No place in the bathroom, except behind the shower curtain. No one there. When I came back from the bathroom, Miss Jadwin had switched on the TV. She fooled around with the dial until she found a news broadcast. They were, of course, talking about Rainbow

Hill. We watched for a minute or two, and then she went off into the bathroom."

"That was the last time you saw her alive?"

Swenson nodded.

"She didn't scream or call out for help?"

Swenson's cheek twitched violently. "The TV was on, but I'd have heard her if she'd raised her voice."

"How long was she in there before you began to wonder?" the reporter asked.

Swenson hesitated. "Five or six minutes, I suppose."

"You're telling us the bathroom was empty, she went in and closed the door. In five minutes or so, the murderer came down a fire ladder, got in the bathroom window, brandished a knife at her, and she didn't scream?"

"I didn't hear a scream, certainly."

"So she's cut to pieces and this guy goes out the window and up his rope ladder—all in five minutes?"

"I guess that's the way it must have been," Swenson said.

"You're supposed to be guarding her, and you let her go in the bathroom and close the door?"

"That's enough," Shannon said angrily. "Swenson had searched the bathroom, there was no one there. The lady goes in and closes the door. What's Swenson supposed to do, go in and hold the toilet paper for her? That's all, gentlemen. We've got more important things to do than answer questions."

The reporters were reluctantly ushered out to join the ones who'd been excluded. Shannon turned to Quist and Garvey. "You two are the last people except Miss Ames to talk with Bev Jadwin. What can you tell me? Was she nervous, scared? Did she believe someone was out to get her?" The captain glanced across the room at Sandra. "Miss Ames is in shock, I guess you'd say. She doesn't give us anything that makes much sense."

"Dan and I don't have anything very positive to tell you,

Shannon," Quist said. "Dan and the two ladies and I were having what I suppose you might call a scientific conversation. Nobody had come up with anything to explain why Patti Payne was killed, what it was she might suddenly have remembered that would expose the killer. Starting with Sandra, these ex-wives cover most of Larry Lewis's adult life. Each one of them had to know special things about the others. We thought if we began at the beginning and talked down the years, we might suddenly hit on something."

"By next Christmas," Shannon said.

"It could have happened in the next sentence, around the very next corner," Quist said.

"But it didn't?"

"No. It hadn't gone on very long when Swenson came to tell Bev you'd given permission for her to get what she'd left in that other room. If it had gone on longer, we might have come onto what we were looking for—but we didn't."

"The ladies couldn't name anyone who had it in for Lewis or who had it in for Glenda Forrest?"

"Larry is still Mr. Wonderful in their book," Garvey said. "Glenda wasn't their favorite woman in the world, but they didn't come up with a big hater."

"Damn!" Shannon said.

"You have to think now, don't you, that someone has set out to do away with Larry Lewis, his past and his present?" Garvey asked.

"We're still, for God's sake, guessing—but yes," Shannon said.

"How do you plan to protect Sandra?" Quist asked.

Shannon was starting to show a kind of exhausted frustration. "I want to take her to the trooper barracks, lock her up there where it would take an army to get at her. Stubborn bitch doesn't want any part of it. We might find Larry somewhere, or he might turn up here alive and well. She

149

wants to be here when either one of those things happens."

"You have the legal right to place her in protective custody, don't you?" Garvey asked.

"You two should know what it's like to deal with famous people," Shannon said. "The Queen of Hollywood with a million fans adoring her down through the years. They'd want me to give her the best protection, but if she complains publicly, my name would be mud. I'm trying to get someone higher up to give me orders. Meanwhile, I thought you might help, Quist. She seems to trust you."

"Do my best," Quist said.

"She's been trying to get in touch with her lawyer, a man named Robinson, who is also Lewis's lawyer. No luck so far."

"Dale Robinson," Garvey said. "Great sports fan, like Larry. Wouldn't he have been in touch when he heard what's happened here?"

"He hasn't been."

"So he hasn't heard," Garvey said. "I could try to get in touch with some friends of mine in the sports world who might know where he is."

"Someplace where they don't have a radio or a TV set?" Shannon asked.

"He may not be an addict," Garvey said. "Fishing or hunting somewhere, maybe on his way home now. Tomorrow is Monday, a business day."

"It's already tomorrow," Shannon said, glancing at his wristwatch. "A quarter past one. Do what you can with the lady, Quist. I'm only trying to do what's best and safest for her. I'll do it anyway when I get the word from the top."

Garvey took off to try to locate the missing lawyer. Quist crossed the room to where Sandra sat, alone and looking older than he remembered. She gave him a puzzled look as he approached.

"Julian?"

150

"Yes, luv, it's Julian." He wondered if her eyesight was faulty. Then he realized how deep the shock of Bev's death must be.

"Thank you for coming," Sandra said, as if she'd sent for him and he'd responded.

"Captain Shannon asked me to explain to you why—"

"I don't want him to hear what I have to tell you, Julian. Is there someplace we can be private?"

"Corner of the room over there," Quist said. "Shannon isn't going to let you out of his sight, luv."

She took his hand and led him to a bench under the far windows that looked out on a starlit night. He was aware that her hand was cold as ice. They sat close together on the bench, and Sandra's voice was no more than a whisper.

"Forty years ago Larry made one of his first big hit comedies. I remember it vividly because that was the film where we met, the one I told you about when he saved me from failure in my first acting try and I—I fell in love with him."

"Sandra, we can't go back to this remembering business now. You have got to be taken somewhere safe, and I—"

"Listen!" Her fingernails bit sharply into his wrist. "It was a film called *The Human Fly*. It was the kind of wacky script Harold Lloyd used to do many, many years ago. Tough on people with phobias. Larry played a comedy crook who climbed the faces of skyscrapers to get into high-up offices to commit his burglaries. Larry did those stunts for real. He wasn't a big star yet, so they let him risk his neck, which they wouldn't have done later."

"Sandra, please. You've got to understand what Shannon—"

"Listen, listen!" Her voice was louder and then reverted to the whisper. "It was made to look as if Larry were climbing up the stone faces of those skyscrapers. The Human Fly. Of course he wasn't. There were rope ladders, carefully painted to match the stonework, not visible to the cameras. It wasn't totally without danger, but it wasn't as dangerous as it looked. He would fake missteps, and watching the film, women would scream. It was marvelously funny, and Larry was on the way up—not the face of a skyscraper, but up the ladder of stardom."

"Fascinating, but what's the point, Sandra?"

"Yesterday, or whenever it was I came here, Larry escorted me to the room I was supposed to occupy. He was in high spirits, with the party coming up and all. He showed me my room and he showed me the rope ladder fire escape that was there, just in case.

"'The Human Fly lives again,' he said, laughing. 'Bring a lover up here, and I may come down the outside of the building and have at him. Believe it or not, I've tried these things and I find I could still be the Human Fly.'"

Quist felt a strange cold chill run over his body. "Are you suggesting, Sandra, that Larry—"

"I'm just telling you, Julian, and I don't want you to tell anyone else. If it was Larry who slipped into Bev's bathroom after the trooper had searched it, if it was Larry who blew up the cottage, if it was Larry who destroyed poor Patti, then I will be next."

"So Shannon's plans for your safety are vital."

She shook her head slowly. "If it is Larry, whatever has driven him to this madness will bring him to me. It will bring him now, or later sometime. If that's the way it is, I don't want to live, Julian. I want to wait for him to come and do it in his own way and in his own time."

"That's crazy!" Quist said.

"It may not be Larry; I hope to God it isn't," Sandra said. "But it could be, could be, could be!" She lowered her head against his shoulder and her whole body shook. "If that's the way it is, I don't want to go on a step further. Let him have his way and be done with it."

"You know I can't let that happen," Quist said.

"If Larry has planned it, you can't stop him," Sandra said. "That's the way he is. And if he's done all these horrible things, I don't want to live knowing it."

Quist's arm was around her, hoping it would give her some comfort. If by any chance her fears were based on fact, it was the end of the world for her. He thought he could understand her wanting to face Larry, if it was Larry, in what would be the last of it for her.

But it couldn't be Larry, he thought. If Larry had determined to punish his "family," surely he'd have found a different way, something unique, not copied after a kind of weird sickness. He was an original, and he'd have chosen an original way to act, even if he'd gone off his rocker.

"If I could prove to you that it's not Larry, Sandra, would you let Shannon—"

"No!"

"You've made up your mind that it's Larry, luv. I'm just as convinced that it isn't. Give me some time to try to prove to you that I'm right. In the meantime, let Shannon protect you in his way so that someone we haven't guessed at yet can't get to you. I don't say you're not in danger, Sandra. I just want a chance to prove to you that Larry isn't that danger."

"Oh, God, if you were only right!" she whispered.

"Give me just a few hours."

After a moment she nodded her head very slowly. "I—I don't believe you can. But if you only could—"

2

Quist had no very clear notion of how to set about proving that it wasn't Larry Lewis who had unleashed the reign of terror at Rainbow Hill. But he had what he supposed could be called a gut feeling about it. Not Larry, no way. How could he satisfy Sandra, teetering on the brink of total despair? He had one notion for a starting point. It had been there, apparently nesting in the back of his brain, ever since the details of Bev Jadwin's brutal finish had begun to circulate. How had the murderer known that Bev would return to her room? How had he known exactly when? He hadn't just gone there to wait for a possible return to the room by Bev. He'd known exactly when, known he must wait until the police had made sure there was no one there before he came down his rope ladder and in through the bathroom window. Anything but exact information ahead of time suggested the most extraordinary piece of blind luck—good luck for the killer, bad luck for Bev.

One thing was certain. Larry couldn't have been present when Shannon gave Trooper Swenson permission to escort Bev to her room. He couldn't have been present, because he couldn't appear anywhere without hundreds of people greeting him joyfully. There was no way he could have been present while any kind of plans were made for anyone.

Captain Shannon was a man who, in the last sixteen hours, had listened to so many wild guesses from so many people that he found himself braced against anything new from anyone.

"Just the same, the possibility that Lewis is the murderer

has been up front from the very beginning," he said when Quist had told him about Sandra's fears. "You ask a question, Quist, how could Lewis have known that Bev Jadwin was going back to her original room to collect some belongings? Let me go back over it. Miss Jadwin called me on the phone from the suite she was sharing with Miss Ames. She'd left things in her first room, and the troopers on guard wouldn't let her go there without permission from me. I'm stretched awfully thin for manpower here, and I told her that as soon as I could free a trooper to go with her I'd let her know. She didn't mention this to you and Garvey when you were up there with her and Miss Ames?"

"We didn't know anything about it until Swenson told her you'd given permission for her to go," Quist said.

"So let's go back to Larry Lewis," Shannon said. "There are phones in every room and every office here in the Inn, all connected through a switchboard. It's not impossible that Lewis, who knows the system, could somehow be plugged in on my line here, listening to everything I say on the phone."

"Then he could have known that Bev was going back to her room?"

"If he could have been plugged in," Shannon said. "But he couldn't have known when! I told Miss Jadwin on the phone I'd let her know when I could spare a man to go with her. I didn't call her back to tell her, I just sent Swenson up to escort her. Swenson and I on our end knew just when, and you and Garvey and Miss Ames knew when Swenson reported up in the suite where you were. That was never on the phone, so it couldn't have been overheard that way."

"Could Bev have told someone who, innocently or otherwise, passed it on to the killer?" Quist asked.

"She couldn't have told anyone when it was going to happen," Shannon said. "She didn't know. I didn't know until a free trooper became available."

"Some kind of miracle in the man's timing," Quist said.

"Down the rope ladder from the room above, *after* Swenson had searched the bathroom, a brutal murder, and up the ladder in the space of five minutes. Everything had to happen exactly right for him."

"So whoever it is, it was a miracle of timing."

"You've been searching for Larry for more than fourteen hours," Quist said. "What are the odds that he is here and you haven't found him?"

Shannon flexed his fingers as though they were stiff from fatigue. Everybody at Rainbow Hill was flirting with exhaustion. "We look for lost people all the time," Shannon said. "It's part of a trooper's job—missing kids, old people who wander off. You search a property, a house and grounds like this Inn and its outbuildings; if the person is dead or not moving around you find him. Maybe the second time, but you find him. Acres of woodland, open country, are something else again. So many places you have no reason to know about—a cave, a deep pool, just brush and leaves that look perfectly natural but are actually covering something. Good dogs, given an old shoe, a piece of clothing that belonged to the missing person, can be very effective. We've had good dogs out there, clothes out of Lewis's golf club locker. Nothing!"

"So you're saying the odds are that Larry isn't anywhere here at Rainbow Hill?"

Shannon flexed his fingers again, looking down at them as though they puzzled him. "I'd make a very substantial bet that Lewis's dead body isn't anywhere in the Inn, or the outbuildings, or the surrounding grounds. I'd make a slightly less substantial bet that his body isn't in the woods. We're going over them for the third time now, and nothing has surfaced."

"So he isn't here at Rainbow Hill," Quist said.

The trooper captain's eyes narrowed. "I don't think he's here dead," Shannon said.

"Are you saying he could be here alive? Alive and invisible?"

"The murderer is obviously alive," Shannon said.

"And you think Larry—?"

"I'm just answering your questions," Shannon said. "He could be here and alive. Not out in the woods, I'd guess. Lewis knows every inch of space in this Inn and the outbuildings. He knew about the dynamite and where it was stored. He knew which was Bev Jadwin's room and what room was directly above it. He was, according to Miss Ames, the Human Fly from years ago. He could have been tuned in on my telephone calls."

"But you've searched the Inn and all the outbuildings over and over."

"So let's say we begin by searching the top floor. He knows from wherever he's hiding that that's where we are. We don't find him. As soon as we leave the third floor he knows we won't be looking there soon again. He goes to the third floor, where he knows he's safe. He's safe until we start a second go-around. Then he goes somewhere else, waits till we've cleared an area or a room, and then goes there for safety again. A man who could plan the murder of Miss Jadwin so skillfully could provide for his own safety with equal skill."

"And you think it's Larry?"

"I said 'a man,'" Shannon said. "Let's face it, Quist, there is every reason in the world to think Larry Lewis is *not* our man. You have to think the bombing of the cottage was meant for him. When he appeared after that and it was obvious he hadn't died in the blast, he disappears. The murderer having missed once tried again? Then a second ex-wife and a third ex-wife are butchered. Three of the four dead people were all close to and cared for by Lewis. McNally, in the cottage with ex-wife number four, was an accident. I don't blame Miss Ames for thinking her number may be up, but unless she's holding out on us, I don't see any reason for her to believe that Larry Lewis is alive and gone berserk."

"Except for the fact that he meets all the requirements," Quist said. "The Human Fly, he knows every crevice and crack of this establishment, he is closely connected with the three murdered women and with the one who's afraid she's next."

"Are you saying you now believe it's Lewis?" Shannon asked.

Quist's smile was thin. "I'm trying to get you to say, flaty, that you don't believe it is, so that I can reassure Sandra. She won't resist any kind of protection if she's convinced it isn't Larry."

"I can't say I know it isn't Lewis," Shannon said, "but I don't think it is. As for the lady, she's right about one thing. She's likely to be next if we don't find out who it is before he can strike. He only has to wait for the right moment— tonight, tomorrow, next month! I want to take her away from here and have someone else protecting her. One more murder right under my nose, and I'll wind up selling shoelaces on the corner."

Quist was silent for a moment. "Do you mind if Garvey and I get ourselves involved all the way in this?"

"The whole damned town is," Shannon said. Then he shook his head. "No, I don't include you guys in that. You won't be in the way. People may talk to you more freely than they'll talk to the law. Play it in the open with me, and I'll be grateful."

"You have any idea where Bobby Crown is?" Quist asked. "He might be helpful with Sandra if he knows what she's thinking."

"He was out on his feet," Shannon said. "When we heard about Miss Jadwin, he just about collapsed. Our doctor gave him something so he could get some sleep. God knows he isn't the only one who needs it." He glanced across the room. "Try to persuade the lady that I'm not the enemy."

There wasn't anything yet to persuade Sandra that her nightmare wasn't real. Quist told her that Shannon was almost certain she was wrong, but the word "almost" was badly chosen. Sandra just stared at him with wide, frightened eyes. She had convinced herself to a point of no return without solid proof. So that kind of solid proof must be found, even if it was Larry's dead body, which had so far escaped the searchers.

All you could do was walk out into the disaster world like a blind man groping for some kind of familiar guidepost. The sight of Garvey walking briskly toward him cheered Quist. In this whole dark climate, Dan was the only sure and certain rock of safety.

"Any luck?" Quist asked.

"Yes and no," Garvey said. "Dale Robinson, Sandra and Larry's lawyer, is on his way. Should be here fairly soon if he isn't arrested for speeding. He'd been on a weekend golfing trip somewhere and heard the news from Rainbow Hill on his car radio. He stopped somewhere, phoned home, and headed directly here."

"He'll probably be some help to Sandra," Quist said, and brought his friend up to date on the lady's horrors.

"You think it could be?" Garvey asked.

"Right now I'm going to try to prove that it isn't," Quist said. "Save Sandra's sanity if I can. I was headed to try to find Bobby Crown, although it's doubtful he can be of much help for a while. Doctor doped him up so he can get some sleep."

"He's up on the third floor, isn't he?" Garvey asked. I'd thought of trying to find out if there was any new evidence in the room where Bev was killed. It's on the way there. I don't know if the cops will open up to us, but—"

"Shannon's given us a green light," Quist said. "Worth a try."

A trooper was guarding the door of the room where Bev had been killed. He told Quist and Garvey that Sloan was inside, in charge. No one to be admitted.

"Ask him if he'll call Captain Shannon about us," Quist said.

The trooper went into the room and a few minutes later a scowling Sloan opened the door and beckoned them in.

"Shannon says you're here to help," the homicide cop said. "I've been sitting here soaking my head, trying to see something I may have missed."

Quist told him about Sandra.

"I was there once, as you know," Sloan said. "Lewis was my first choice."

"Not anymore?" Garvey asked.

"'The music goes round and round,'" Sloan said. "What have we got? The room just above this on the third floor is where the killer came from. No doubt about that. The rope fire ladder from that room is up there, but the killer didn't take time to fold it up and put it away. Just dropped it on the floor. There are fresh scratches on the windowsill there where the ladder was hooked to lower him down. The damned rope ladder won't take fingerprints, and what prints we've found up there don't seem to be related. A bathroom glass, the bureau—nothing on the windowsill. Could be the maid's, or the man's who occupied the room earlier."

"Who was he?"

"Party guest, a movie actor named Mike Reid. He was one of the first ones released by Shannon yesterday morning. We checked him out. He's in New York, where he lives. Wasn't within a hundred and fifty miles of here when Bev Jadwin was killed."

"The killer had to know that this was Bev Jadwin's room,"

Quist said, "that she was coming here, and that Reid's room was just above it."

"Lewis could have known all that, of course. So could a dozen other people, the maids, the staff, other guests."

"What puzzles me," Garvey said, "is how the killer could risk going down that rope ladder on the outside of the building with all kinds of people moving around in the yard below, searchlights in the garden. He would have had the greatest kind of luck not to have been spotted."

"The windows here in this bedroom open out onto the garden where people were," Sloan said. "But the bathroom is around the corner of the building. The window there opens onto an inside courtyard. Nobody there. He went from the bathroom window above it to the bathroom window below. You may not want to look in the bathroom. We haven't cleaned anything up there yet."

"No screen on the window?" Garvey asked. "It's summertime."

"There's a sliding screen. It was up when we found her. The killer didn't stop to close it when he left. He was in a hurry. He knew Swenson was in the next room and would be calling out to the lady when she didn't show."

"There is something that I need to have explained," Quist said. "Bev went into the bathroom and closed the door. Maybe she was going to use the facilities, maybe it was just automatic—you go into a bathroom and you close the door. Swenson had searched the place a couple of minutes before. No one. He said Bev watched the TV for a couple of minutes and then she went in. Now, with Bev in there, the killer lifts up the screen, climbs through the window, and attacks her. And she doesn't open her mouth to call for help?"

"I've been there, too," Sloan said bitterly. "He could have been hanging outside on his rope ladder, got the screen up after Swenson had searched. Or he could have

161

gotten that screen up before they ever came to the room and was waiting outside, hanging on his ladder."

"Did Swenson notice whether the screen was up when he searched?"

"He doesn't remember," Sloan said. "He was looking for someone who might be hiding there. He hadn't thought of the possibility of someone coming in a second-story window. But it doesn't really matter. The killer could have opened the screen ahead of time and been hanging on his rope ladder outside, or he could have opened it when Swenson left and then come in."

"The screen would make some noise going up, wouldn't it?" Garvey asked.

"Yes, it makes some kind of a scratching sound. But with that damned TV set going—" Sloan shrugged. "I have to believe the screen was open when Swenson searched. The minute he was gone, the killer came in off his ladder, hid behind the shower curtain, and Bev Jadwin never knew what hit her, didn't have a chance to scream. Then—up and away."

"Patti Payne was murdered in a room just down the hall from this one," Quist said. "You weren't guarding this area?"

"We had a man in the hall," Sloan said. "As a matter of fact, all four ex-wives had adjoining rooms on this corridor. I suppose it was set up that way because they were friends. Unfortunately, none of us thought of the Human Fly."

"Lewis?" Garvey asked.

"A twelve-year-old boy could handle those rope ladders."

"That's about Larry's size, isn't it—a twelve-year-old boy," Quist said. "How big is that screen opening?"

Sloan's eyes darkened. "A big man would have had a hell of a time squeezing through," he said.

Garvey glanced at Quist. "The more you back away, the closer you get," he said.

"Meaning what?" Sloan asked.

"Julian and I set out to prove that it couldn't have been Larry, partly because, knowing him, we don't believe it could be, and partly to assure Miss Ames that the killer isn't the man she cares about so much and has cared about for so long. But"—Garvey shrugged—"everything we learn about the killer seems to aim straight at Larry. Agile on the rope ladder—the Human Fly. Complete knowledge of the geography of this plant—Larry. Only a little guy could get in and out of that bathroom window in a hurry—Larry. So maybe we should stop backing away and go for the jugular."

"We have to find him first," Quist said.

"So we need someone who knows the plant and the surrounding countryside as well as Larry does," Quist said. "I suppose Bobby Crown, who's doped out at the moment. Ricardo? He's been here preparing for a couple of weeks."

"The contractor who remodeled the Inn for Larry," Garvey said.

"Bill McGee, local guy—if you wanted a guided tour. There's one other possibility. Madge Seaton," Sloan said.

"The gal Larry spent the end of the party night with?" Garvey asked.

Sloan's smile was sour. "In her guest room, remember. From the first day Lewis saw this property, she was always with him. She has blueprints of the place, took Lewis over every inch of it while she was trying to make a sale."

"She might remember what interested him, intrigued him," Garvey said. "She's been closer to Larry than she would like us to think—I think. Could even be helping him hide, as she did after the party. She's worth a try, don't you think, Julian?"

Quist looked at his wristwatch. "After two A.M."

"You wouldn't wake the lady up to save a life?" Garvey asked. "I'm talking about Sandra's life."

"Let's go," Quist said.

Quist and Garvey didn't get to the Seatons' house across

the way as quickly as they'd expected. As they went down the stairs in the lobby, a big man with iron-gray hair and a bulldog jaw was just coming in the front entrance.

"Dan!" he called out, as he saw Garvey.

"It's Dale Robinson, the lawyer," Garvey explained to Quist. "Got here sooner than I expected."

"Thank the Lord you're here," Robinson said. His handshake was bone-crushing when he was introduced to Quist. "What kind of a slaughterhouse is this, anyway?"

The lobby was almost deserted now except for trooper traffic. The three men sat together in a comfortable corner while Garvey took Dale Robinson down the horror path, from the blasted cottage to the murder of Bev Jadwin. Quist wrapped it up with an account of Sandra Ames's current nightmare. The big lawyer listened without interruption or questions until they got into the theory that Larry Lewis was the killer.

"There's one thing the three of us don't need," Robinson said. "We don't need proof that Larry is innocent. We know that. I've handled his business and personal affairs for more than twenty years. He's a very special, very different, very unusual kind of guy, but a psychotic killer? Never! Out to butcher his four ex-wives? Absurd!"

"When somebody flips, he's no longer the person you know," Garvey said. "You might know of some pressures he was under that we don't, pressures that could turn him from good to bad, from white to black."

"What possible pressures?" Robinson asked. "His whole life is a success story."

"Except for his marriages," Quist said.

"I don't think he thought of them as failures, except possibly Glenda," Robinson said. "They were relationships he remembered with pleasure. He kept the women as friends when the marriages ended. He had no financial problems with any of them. He made one settlement on

164

each of them when the game was over, paid no alimony, nothing to bother him economically. I know there was a stretch when Sandra had money troubles. Larry helped her. Later she paid him back, every dime. He used his influence to help their careers—except Glenda, who didn't have one and didn't need help. It may be unusual, but I never heard Larry say a word about his ex-wives that wasn't affectionate and caring."

"But he flipped," Garvey said.

"I simply don't buy that," Robinson said. "He's in big trouble somewhere, but he hasn't flipped. Bet on it."

"Something about this venture here at Rainbow Hill?" Garvey said, not giving in.

"He's in love with this place," Robinson said. "We had a lot of talk about it because it cost him so much. I had to be the devil's advocate when he was considering it. It was going to cost him a couple of million bucks to buy the property, remodel the plant, equip and supply it. It wasn't a business venture to him. You know why he wanted to do it?"

Quist shook his head.

"He'd spent a big part of his life on the road, traveling with shows, living in hotels from one end of the country to the other. He told me he used to lie in bed in some of those fleabags where he had to stay, dreaming of the perfect hotel somewhere that would have everything for the guest that you can imagine. So there came a time when he could afford to make his dream come true." Robinson smiled. "You know one reason I'm sure Larry can't be your killer? He would never have blown up that cottage. He loves every brick and blade of grass on this place. If he was going to kill somebody, he wouldn't have damaged his dream place in the process. Look, gentlemen, we can't just sit here talking. We've got to find Larry. He's in big trouble somewhere."

"I wish you'd talk to Sandra, sell her some of your convictions about Larry," Quist said.

"Where is she?" the lawyer asked.

"Take him to her, will you, Dan?" Quist said. "I'd like to go across the street and talk to the Seatons. There's just a chance Madge Seaton may have something that will be helpful."

3

There were lights burning in the windows of the Seatons' house. It was well after two in the morning but someone was still up.

Quist rang the front doorbell and waited. The top half of the door was glass with a curtain drawn over it. The curtain was parted and Madge Seaton looked out. Then the door opened.

"Mr. Quist!"

"This is an ungodly hour, I know," Quist said. "Somehow what's been going on has destroyed my awareness of the time of day. I needed to talk to you and your husband, and I just came."

Madge Seaton was wearing a pale pink housecoat. She was a small woman, just the right size for Larry, Quist thought.

"Howard has gone back to Ohio," Madge Seaton said. There was a bitter tone in her voice. "Shannon decided he couldn't hold my husband as a murder suspect, so he let him go back to his job. Come in, Mr. Quist."

She indicated a highbacked wing chair, offered him coffee or a drink. "How can I help? Is there something new?"

"Not since Bev Jadwin. Of course, Larry has disappeared into thin air, and that's really why I'm here."

"I don't understand." Madge said, her eyes narrowing.

"I'm glad your husband isn't here, Madge," Quist said. "I was trying to figure out a way to ask you things if he was here. So I don't have to play games. You and I know that Larry didn't spend the time after the party in your guest room."

"That's where he was," Madge said, her voice brittle.

"I'm not a cop or a reporter," Quist said. "Whatever we talk about won't go onto an official record, or appear in any headline or gossip column. Whether Larry was just a business associate of yours, or a friend, or if he was your lover, Madge, we have—I hope—a mutual concern. We would both like to help Larry, save him from what may be a mortal danger at the hands of a madman."

"What difference does it make what my relationship with Larry has been?" she asked.

"A business associate isn't likely to share his intimate personal life with you; there may be things you wouldn't tell the best of friends. But a lover? That wonderful, relaxed, and tender time after you've made love is when there are no secrets. I want to ask you, in such moments, what Larry may have told you about his dreams, his ambitions, his anxieties, about his ex-wives whom you were to meet at the party. Three of them are suddenly dead, Madge, and the fourth is waiting in terror for it to be her turn. She and others think we may be dealing with Larry gone crazy."

"Oh, no!"

"If we could forget trying to pretend that you and Larry were just business associates, we might be able to get something that would help him."

She sat silent for a moment, her fingers locked so tightly together in her lap that her knuckles were white. "I love my husband very much," she said finally. "It isn't a romance out of a novel, but it has been a tender, sharing, happy partnership. I would rather die than hurt him."

"But you did take a lover."

"You are a very attractive man, Mr. Quist. If you were to make a pass at me I'd be flattered, but I'd say no. But Larry—! He was a stranger, yet not a stranger. I'd grown up on his films. I knew him, just the way other girls must feel they know Cary Grant, although they've never actually seen him in the flesh." She shook her head. "This strange, marvelous little man had been married to four glamorous women, and involved with goodness knows how many more. He must have something extra special to offer."

"And he made a pass at you?"

Madge nodded. "It's silly, but I thought that pass was just his way of being polite to someone who was helping him buy a property. Automatic, I thought, like holding a lady's dining-room chair for her, or taking off his hat to you when he meets you on the street. But the pass came again." She lowered her eyes. "Howard was away in Ohio. It couldn't hurt him. I wasn't going to fall in love. But there it was, little Madge Seaton in a small New England town approached by one of the world's great lovers. It was like trying to decide whether you'll go on a high ride at the county fair. I was tempted, and I went for the ride." She lowered her eyes. "It wasn't a question of being in love or of breaking up my marriage. I just went for the ride. It—it was pretty sensational."

"So you went for the ride again."

"I didn't intend to. I'd had a rare experience, and that was that. But all he had to do was touch me with a finger and it turned on my motor. I—I became an addict. Larry never approached me when Howard was at home, never asked me to make a choice, but when we were free to make love—we made love."

168

"Those are the times when he could have talked to you freely about himself, his past, other women," Quist said.

She almost laughed. "I remember one thing he said to me once. 'Famous sayings that aren't true—all cats are alike in the dark. Not true, angel. Each of you are marvelous in your own way, given an imaginative approach.' Imaginative approaches are Larry's stock-in-trade, I guess."

"He talked about the ex-wives?"

"I was curious about them when I heard they were all coming to the party," Madge said. "Of course Sandra was another film star I'd grown up on. I'd seen Bev and Patti on the stage in New York. Glenda was just someone in the magazines—rich heiress who'd had a brief whirl at marriage with him. It surprised me that they were all coming to the party. 'Best friends,' Larry told me. Glenda wasn't quite in that category, he told me, but he was 'working at it.'"

"Anyone else he spoke of as close to him?"

"Bobby Crown, of course," Madge said. "He thinks of Bobby as a sort of younger brother. Depends on him for so much. I have reason to think he has no secrets from him."

"What reason?"

She looked uncomfortable. "Bobby made a pass at me. He obviously knew that Larry and I had been playing games, thought I might be available. I just laughed at him. I told Larry later. It was right here in this room. He started to do a little tap dance and I recognized the tune—'Anything you can do I can do better—No you can't, yes I can, no you can't.'—'Poor Bobby, always trying to match me at everything,' Larry said. 'I've tried to teach him, but he just doesn't have what it takes.'"

Quist sat very still for a moment. "Did he suggest to you that Bobby had ever made passes at any of his other women?"

"I asked him, and he just laughed and said, 'There's only one king of the midgets.' He always laughs at his small size.

169

He might have been bitter about it, I suppose, if it hadn't made him a fortune."

"Did you take it from that that Bobby *had* made passes at the ex-wives?"

"I took it to mean that he might have, but that if he had, they, like me, had laughed at him. 'There's only one king of the midgets.'"

"Larry wasn't angry at Bobby for making a pass at you?"

"He adores Bobby," Madge said. "He's said many times that he couldn't get along without him. He was almost like a proud papa about the pass at me—proud of his kid for making a try at something, proud even though that something was out of reach."

"Bobby never tried again?"

"Just the once."

Quist stood up. "I think I owe you, Madge. Look, I'm going back to the Inn. I want you to lock your doors and stay alert until I can send someone to keep you safe, or I know that you're safe."

"Safe from what?" Madge asked.

"A disturbed killer who may also have you on his hit list," Quist said.

It was like the sun breaking through a bank of clouds. Bobby Crown! So many things fell into place. Only a little man could have squeezed through the bathroom window in Bev Jadwin's room. Bobby had been Larry's stand-in in early films, his double in size. Larry had played games with the fire-escape ladders, the Human Fly. Bobby had probably played along with him. The four ex-wives could have been a part of Bobby's life, too. Had he made a play for them and been laughed at, as he had in the case of Madge Seaton? That could drive a sick mind into a frenzy, launch the man into the slaughter of all the people who'd laughed at him. Larry? Would he also have harmed Larry, who was his whole life? Not impossible if Larry teased him about his failures. "Anything you can do I can do better"! It could be just another guess, another dream, but deep down in his gut, Quist was grimly certain that it wasn't. This was it.

The Inn seemed almost deserted. The office was empty except for one trooper who'd been part of Shannon's staff earlier in the evening. Sandra was gone.

"Captain Shannon?" Quist asked.

"He's taken the lady over to the barracks for safekeeping," the trooper said. "Your friend Garvey and her lawyer friend went with them."

"Inspector Sloan, Mr. Martin?"

"People have to get forty winks sometime," the trooper said. "They've been going around the clock."

"Can you put me through to the barracks, get me on to Shannon?"

"I can try," the trooper said. He dialed a number. "Mac? Joe Connolly here. Can I talk to the captain?" Pause, and then to Quist: "The captain has gone into the sleep tank, too."

"Miss Ames—is there a phone where she's being held?"

Connolly asked and got an answer. "No dice," he said.

"Is she safe? Is she all right?"

Another question and an answer. "A tank corps couldn't get at her, Mr. Quist."

"I'm going up to talk to Bobby Crown," Quist said. "If Shannon or Sloan gets in touch tell them it's important they join me."

"Little guy's trying to get some shut-eye," the trooper said. "I understand the doc gave him somethiing to help him sleep."

"Well, I can try," Quist said. "His room's on the third floor, I believe. You know which one it is?"

Connolly glanced at a pad on his desk. "Got everyone here we might need in a hurry. Room three B."

Perhaps it was foolish to go about this alone, but, prepared, Quist felt certain he could handle Bobby Crown, butcher knife and all.

He climbed the two flights of stairs to the third floor and knocked on the door of 3B, loudly in case Bobby was really asleep. The door was opened almost at once, and a haggard Bobby Crown looked out at him.

"Julian! What the hell—?"

"Like to talk, Bobby."

"I'm about talked to death, Julian," Bobby said. "But come in. The doctor gave me something to help me sleep. It hasn't worked, but it's left me feeling a little fuzzy." He shook his head as if he were trying to clear it.

Quist looked around the room. The bed was rumpled. Bobby was dressed, pants, sports shirt, shoes, so he'd evidently tried to nap that way under a light summer blanket. Quist looked at the two windows and saw that the screen was up on one of them.

"I see you've got a screen up," Quist said. "That so you can do your Human Fly act at will?"

Bobby frowned at the window. "I had it up awhile back to demonstrate to Captain Shannon how our fire ladders work," he said. "Guess I forgot to close it."

"Let's get right down to business, Bobby. What have you done to Larry?"

"What do you mean, what have I done?" Bobby said. He reached out to the bureau as if he needed to brace himself.

"Did he get on your hit list because he teased you about the ladies who laughed at you?"

"You know damn well I wouldn't do anything to hurt Larry!" Bobby said. He faced the bureau and lowered his head on his arms.

"I thought that all day, Bobby, but now I know about the ladies! I wouldn't be facing you alone if Sandra weren't safe. They have taken her to the trooper barracks. Or did you know?"

Bobby made a kind of choking sound. He opened the top drawer of the bureau and then turned to face Quist. He was holding a .45 caliber handgun, aimed directly at Quist's chest.

"So Sandra talked," he said.

"What's the matter, Bobby, no butcher knife this time?" Quist asked, trying to keep the cold fear he felt from sounding in his voice.

"I don't take any chances wrestling with a big guy like you," Bobby said. He slipped past the bureau to the door, holding the gun steadily on Quist. He locked the door and fastened the inside chain lock in place.

"Sandra didn't talk," Quist said.

"Then it must have been Madge Seaton," Bobby said. He nodded toward the windows. "I saw you going across the street to her house. I didn't think she'd talk, little slut trying to keep her marriage going while she's in the hay with Larry."

"You know that the cops have just about pinned this whole thing on Larry," Quist said. "I suddenly figured that you would fill all the specifications: imitating Larry's Human Fly skills, a little guy crawling through a little bathroom window, interested in the same women."

The phone rang.

"Just let it ring," Bobby said. "They'll think I've gone somewhere." His smile glittered. "I'm free to go anywhere, you know? Let me warn you, if they come up here looking for you or me, you keep your mouth shut or I'll blow you to pieces."

"So that will be that," Quist said. "It doesn't matter which murder they get you for. They can only hang you once."

"I know," Bobby said, his face twisted into a crooked caricature of himself. "But before I finish you, I need to tell you—I need to tell someone—what it's all about."

"I know what it's all about," Quist said. He could feel a

173

cold sweat trickling down his back. "You can't dance as well as Larry, you can't sing as well as Larry, you couldn't charm the same women that Larry charmed, you couldn't bear to be laughed at. Have I left something out?"

Bobby moistened his lips. "You left out the most important thing. I did make one of the women. I did, I did!"

"A gold star for effort," Quist said. "What happened? Did she still laugh at you? Were you that inept at the job?"

"You wouldn't know how that would feel, would you, you big, handsome galoot. I wasn't inept! I was good. I was as good as Larry ever was. She would tell you that if she could."

"She?"

"Glenda! Who the hell else but Glenda? Glenda would say yes to anyone, even poor little Bobby Crown! But she let me come back—and back. She flattered me, she told me, 'Don't be late,' when I'd call her to make a date. And then—then one day she just told me to go peddle my papers. She was bored with me, she said. If I wanted to learn how to be sexually fascinating I should take lessons from the master, meaning Larry. I was as good as he is, I know that. What is it he can do that's so marvelous that any other man can't do?"

"So Glenda gave you the gate," Quist said, his eyes focused on the gun that was pointed directly at him. Bobby's hand was steady except when he got steamed up over what he was saying. Then it shook, and Quist prayed, silently, that it wasn't a hair-trigger job. Bobby's wild eyes told Quist that he was dealing with a madman. Any sudden move, and Bobby would squeeze that trigger. Keep him talking, perhaps supply a little sympathy, and Bobby might be talked out of it. "You aren't the only one Glenda's waved off," he said. "Even Larry couldn't make it last with her."

"It was the other way around with them," Bobby said. "Larry walked out on her. I realized later that's why she let

174

me make love to her. Larry would know, or she would tell him if he didn't, tell him that poor miserable little Bobby Crown was as good as he was."

"Did Larry tell you he knew?" Quist asked. Keep him talking!

"He told me. He told me to get out of town fast. He said I should remember what happens to kids who play with matches."

"You didn't take his advice?"

"I didn't have any choice. I couldn't let go of it, and Glenda wouldn't let me have it. Was Larry helping me, or had I found another teacher who might make it worth a girl's while to look at me? She stuck the knife in me every chance she had. And then came the final twist of that knife that made up my mind."

"The last twist?"

"She asked me to set up a place here at Rainbow Hill where she could entertain a lover without her father's man, Paul Powers, knowing about it. I was to arrange it so she could have some other man, not me. I just turned and ran. Then just before the party was to start last night, Larry came to me, half laughing. Glenda had asked *him* to set up a place for her, and he'd given her the cottage. He just told me because he thought it was funny. He thought I was through with Glenda long ago, that I'd taken his advice." Bobby's lips trembled. "She was going to shame me right under my nose! That was the end. She wasn't going to laugh at me anymore. I tried to figure out how to do it. I couldn't charge into the cottage and kill her with that big lug of a chauffeur and bodyguard with her. He could handle me with one hand tied behind him. I couldn't use this—" Bobby waved the gun dangerously "—not with a couple of hundred people all around. Then I remembered the dynamite in the toolshed down by the swimming pool. I could blow them up, right in the middle of their lovemaking!"

"You knew how to handle dynamite?" Quist asked. "I wouldn't have known how."

"When I was a kid I worked as a helper to a building contractor in my hometown," Bobby said. "I watched blasting set up a hundred times. I knew how."

"But with people all around—"

Bobby's smile was that of a cunning conspirator. "They actually helped. No one questioned anyone walking around anywhere. No one was interested in the swimming pool. I had a key to the lock on the chest where the dynamite was stored, but after I had the dynamite ready to move, I broke the lock so nothing would point to me. I carried the stuff over to the cottage and began planting it around the foundation of the cottage. I didn't have to worry about noise. There was the orchestra going in the main building here, people laughing and singing." Bobby's face twitched. "I didn't have to worry about noise at the cottage. That bitch had Larry's stereo going. She likes to make love to music. So I set it up, and when the time came I blew it!" He let his breath out in a long sigh.

There was a sharp knock on the door of the room. "Crown! Open up!" It was Shannon's voice.

Bobby moved quickly around behind Quist, who could feel the cold barrel of the gun against his head.

"One peep out of you, Quist, and it's all over!" Bobby whispered.

Louder knocking. "Crown! Open up!" More knocking, and then Shannon's voice again, quite clear. "He must have gone somewhere."

"Quist was with him." Trooper Connolly's voice.

"So they both went somewhere," Shannon said.

Voices faded away down the corridor.

"Good boy," Bobby said, the gun still held against Quist's head.

"Did you plan to kill the other three women right from

176

the start?" Quist asked, surprised at how cool he could make his voice sound.

"Not really," Bobby said. "I—I was fond of them all. But Patti—she'd been talking to Bev and Sandra in the lobby and was headed for her room. When I saw her she had started up the stairs. 'You must not be feeling too unhappy,' she said. 'From your angle, Glenda must have got what was coming to her.' Then I knew how it was going to be. Larry had no secrets from Patti and Bev and Sandra. He must have told them about my troubles with Glenda. Right now they didn't dream I could be involved, but sooner or later—"

"They'd remember and talk?"

Bobby nodded. "I walked upstairs with Patti, trying to figure out what to do. Outside one of the rooms was a service wagon. Someone, probably one of the reporters, had had dinner served in his room and then pushed the wagon out into the hall, not wanting to be bothered when the room service waiter came for it. There was a steak knife lying on a platter. I—I slipped it under my jacket."

"You hated Patti that much?"

"She had laughed at me once, too—when I'd asked her," Bobby said. "She'd probably told Bev and Sandra. And Bev had laughed at me when I asked her."

"And Sandra?"

"She was too old, but she'd certainly been told by the others. Poor, laughable little Bobby Crown! But they'd put two and two together, sooner or later."

"So you killed Patti?"

"It was quick. She didn't suffer much."

"Brother!" He found it hard to ask. "The tongue?"

"At the moment I thought it was a message that Bev and Sandra would understand. Later I realized it wouldn't stop them. They were moved from their rooms into a suite together, which made it more difficult for me. You were with them. But I was in Shannon's office when Bev phoned down to ask him to let her go back to her original room for things she'd left there. Nobody paid any attention to me. I was one of the good guys. I went up to the room above Bev's, went down the rope ladder to the bathroom window, raised the screen, and waited on the outside, just above the window. I heard them come in, heard Swenson search the bathroom. The minute he was gone I climbed through the window and stood inside the shower curtain. Bev came in, closed the door—and that was that."

"So Sandra is next?"

"It doesn't look like it now," Bobby said. "It looks like you're next, Quist. I had to get this off my chest to someone, but you're next."

Quist was suddenly turned to cold stone. Bobby was behind him, facing the door. He himself was facing the window with the screen up. There was a face there, a face he couldn't believe. Larry Lewis was looking in at him. The little movie star made an imperative gesture of silence—moved his mouth as if to tell Quist to keep talking.

"There must be some way, Bobby, for you and me to come to a better solution," Quist heard himself saying. "Killing me isn't going to get you off the hook. A little silence from me would be little enough to pay for my life. I think I could persuade Sandra not to tell her story. I think—"

Larry Lewis had slipped through the window and was in the room. Suddenly, a grotesque charade began. Larry was tap-dancing and singing.

> "Anything you can do I can do better,
> I can do anything better than you.
> No you can't,
> Yes I can,
> No you can't,
> Yes I can, yes I can, yes I can!"

178

Bobby had spun around. On the last tap note of the song, Larry launched a high karate kick that knocked the gun out of Bobby's hand and up toward the ceiling.

"Yes, I can, boy, yes I can," Larry said in a strange, harsh voice. "Open the door, Julian."

Quist wasn't sure he could move, but he managed it, took the chain off the door, and unlocked it. Shannon, Sloan, and a couple of troopers charged in.

Ahead of them, Bobby Crown had gone to Larry, thrown his arms around him. It was not an attack but an embrace. Larry pushed him sharply away.

"The time for caring ended longer ago than I like to think, Bobby," he said. He turned away as Shannon snapped handcuffs on Bobby's wrists, behind his back.

Larry Lewis was a shattered little man, not a famous movie star, as he sat in Shannon's office surrounded by the law, by Quist and Garvey, by Sandra, who sat beside him holding his hand in hers, and by Dale Robinson. He had lost four close friends and his dream toy, Rainbow Hill, in the space of a few hours. Quist wondered which hurt him the most, the murders of his three ex-wives or the sick treachery of a cherished friend, Bobby Crown. Maybe separate hurts but equal.

Quist gathered from snatches of talk that someone had gotten his message to Shannon, and the trooper had come back from the barracks to Rainbow Hill. As he got out of his car in the parking lot, he had been approached by Larry Lewis, thought to be dead, suspected of murder.

Larry had figured out the answers for himself. Bobby was it. Shannon told him he was on his way to answer a summons from Quist who was, supposedly, in conversation with Bobby at the time.

"I warned him the man was wild, crazy," Larry said. "Break into the room, and we'd probably have a murder-suicide added to things. I suggested they get his attention from the hall and I'd try my Human Fly act from the outside. Fortunately he already had the screen up."

"So it worked," Shannon said. "There hasn't been time, Lewis, to ask you where the hell you've been."

Larry's story was hard to take in. He had, in effect, been kidnapped by Fred Forrest, Glenda's father. The millionaire's private detective had forced him at gunpoint into Forrest's limousine. Since they were free to go, they weren't checked, and Larry was driven away, right past the trooper guards.

"I was responsible for Glenda's death, the old man thought," Larry said. "He was going to be judge, jury, and executioner. I was driven to New York, forced into his lavish townhouse, and there I've been. Third degree, some pretty incredible rough stuff, and all the time the radio and television were going, telling us of new horrors here. The old man was convinced that I was part of it all until we heard the awful news about Bev." Larry shuddered. "That's when I began to put it together. Bobby had made it with Glenda, tried to make it with Patti and Bev. It was straight-line clear to me. He'd gone crazy and was knocking off everyone who'd said no to him. I finally persuaded Forrest to turn me loose and let me get here to stop Bobby."

"You can charge him with kidnapping and collect a few oil wells," Dale Robinson said.

Larry shook his head. "I know, better than I could have the day before yesterday, how he felt about the murder of his daughter. If I'd been here when I knew that Bobby was responsible for Glenda and for Patti, I might have killed him without waiting for you, Shannon. I'm not charging old man Forrest with anything. I know how it was with him." He looked at Robinson. "You can put this place on the market, Dale. Anyone who'll take it off my hands for a nickel can have it. I never want to lay eyes on it again. Can I get out of here now, Shannon?"

"Come with me, darling," Sandra said.

Larry gave her a long look. "Can it be, Sandy, that we need each other again?"

Quist watched them go out together, arm in arm, and silently wished them luck. He, too, never wanted to lay eyes on Rainbow Hill again.